TEMPEST OUTPOST

BRAD HARMER-BARNES

SEVERED PRESS
HOBART TASMANIA

TEMPEST OUTPOST

ISBN: 978-1-925711-25-7

For anyone who has ever attended a Bad Movie Night.

ONE

Jazmin Hayes shivered in her seat as the UH-60 Black Hawk powered through the night sky towards Tempest Outpost. At just nineteen years old, riding an ex-military helicopter across the sea off the coast of Antarctica was one of the most exciting things she had ever done. The cold took the edge off of the thrill somewhat, but it was – nonetheless – an experience.

She smiled across at her co-passenger, Claire Flynn, who was accompanying her to her internship. The representative of Icecap Industries was probably only five years or so older than Jazmin, but those five years seemed to make her a grown woman, whereas Jazmin still felt very much like a teenager loose in an adult world.

"You must be excited?" Claire shouted over the roar of the Black Hawk's rotors, her English accent thankfully making her more understandable. "Six weeks on an experimental drilling rig. With this on your CV you should have the pick of universities, colleges, apprenticeships…whatever you want. You name it, and you'll get on it."

Jazmin was pleased. She'd been fascinated by geology ever since a family holiday to England's coast had led to her finding some fossils on the beach. They weren't exactly dinosaur bones – just some plant imprints – but it had been enough to engage her interest for life. To her, the entire history of the Earth was imprinted in the rock, waiting to be read.

"Yeah, I can't wait! So, have you met the crew before? What are they like?"

"I've met Anna Morris – the expedition leader – a few times over the years. She's a strong woman. Very friendly, but she definitely doesn't take any shit either. I think you'll get along just fine."

"Anyone else?"

"I've met Cameron Barnett in passing. He's the one who designed the Prospero. A very bright guy, but his head's up in the clouds a lot of the time. He's definitely a dreamer, but as an inventor, I suppose you have to be."

Jazmin blinked and wiped her face as a gust of wind brought salt spray in through the half-open side door. "How many crew are there?"

"Six. Including the two I just mentioned. And us two."

"You're staying on?"

Claire grimaced. "I'm afraid so. I'm not just your chauffeur. Every nine months Icecap Industries sends someone along to check that the facility is up to code, and that work's actually being carried out. Essentially I'm just checking that they're not pissing our money away."

"You think they are?"

"Probably not while Morris is in charge, but who knows what we'll find when we get there."

The light inside the passenger compartment switched from a dull yellow to an ominous red, and the co-pilot's voice buzzed through a barely functioning intercom. "Ten minutes to landing."

Jazmin suppressed a shiver. She didn't mind shivering in the cold, but didn't want to show any of her co-workers how nervous she was.

***

Anna Morris and Kurt Townsend, the Geologist, stood on Tempest Outpost's helipad, scanning the sky for signs of the supply chopper. Strands of Anna's blonde hair blew loose from her hat and flew across her eyes. She cursed and squeezed them back under its knitted band.

"You think they'll have burgers on board? I haven't had a decent cheeseburger in four months."

Kurt harrumphed a laugh. A portly German man, he didn't joke about much, and he certainly didn't joke about food. "Maybe. Let's hope they have cheese, too."

"I put in a request for cheese. Cheese and Twinkies."

"Do Twinkies work on a cheeseburger?"

"Twinkies work with anything, Kurt."

Another harrumphed laugh. "I think I see them. Over there."

Anna looked to where the geologist was pointing and couldn't help smiling to herself. "Yeah, unless there are two helicopters fifty miles out from Antarctica, I think that's them. Okay, don't forget to be on your best behaviour around the inspector. She's around until the next supply drop in six weeks. And make sure everyone's on best behaviour with the intern as well. A teenage kid on a drilling rig for six weeks is a recipe for chaos in more ways than one."

"Yes, Captain."

They both flinched away from the gusts of water and ice that span across the helipad as the Black Hawk finally touched down, only relaxing as the rotors finally came to a stop. They made their way carefully across the wet, slippery ground and Anna extended her hand to the older of the two visitors.

"Claire! It's good to see you again. I was worried Icecap were going to send us a tedious old man like the last time. You ever had to talk about cricket for six weeks solid? I'm surprised I didn't go full Jack Torrance on that stretch."

Claire smiled and shook her hand back. "Captain, this is Jazmin Hayes. She's your intern until the next supply chopper comes by. Make sure you show her a little bit of everything."

Anna took in the small young woman in front of her. Her eyes displayed a nervousness that the rest of the face was trying desperately to hide. "Pleased to meet you. You know what we're about here?"

"Uh, drilling and...no, not really. I was just told you were a drilling rig."

Anna tutted at Claire. "You guys really need to sort out your briefings. How about we head out of the cold while your goons unload the supplies? Kurt, you can make sure everything gets sent to the right place."

"I find any Twinkies and I'll be eating them all."

"You do and you'll be going for a swim. Come on, girls, let me show you around."

Anna led Claire and Jazmin through a drafty wooden door and into a cloakroom warmed by two electric fan heaters. Although the room was probably still below twenty degrees, it felt tropical by comparison. They all shucked their heavy winter coats and followed Claire through another door, down a corridor and into a small canteen area. They helped themselves to tea and coffee, and sat at a Formica table.

"Okay", began Anna. "Welcome to Tempest Outpost. I'm Anna Morris, but everyone about Tempest Outpost calls me Captain. I'm not actually a captain, but for the duration of your stay, I'll be the one in charge. You already met Kurt up on the helipad, he's our Geologist. Any rocks or strata that Prospero brings up, he'll be the one leading the analysis. He has an assistant, Bobby. You'll meet him pretty soon, I'm sure."

"What is Prospero?" interrupted Jazmin.

Anna let the silence hang for a moment to show her disapproval, but moved on without further comment. The intern had flushed red with embarrassment at her own rudeness – she was just excited and nervous, that was all. "The Prospero is the drill that this entire rig is built around. Cameron Barnett – again, he's hovering around here somewhere – designed a new shape of drill, which is designed to be able to crack through the rock around here with ease. We should be able to take geological samples that have previously been unobtainable."

"What sort of samples are you looking for?" asked Claire.

Anna shrugged. "New fossils, geological data, alien cities buried beneath the ice; who knows? There could even be crude oil. Don't worry, Miss Flynn. There'll be something to satisfy Icecap's balance sheet or investors or whatever."

"What is it about the rock around here that requires the Prospero?" asked Jazmin.

"We don't really know. All previous attempts with standard equipment have either resulted in very little progress, or in the drills themselves being damaged. So, when Mr Barnett pitched his idea to Icecap, they practically bit his hand off to get it here."

The door leading deeper into the rig banged open and two people in dirty overalls stamped in, laughing with each other. They realised how loud they were being, and waved an apology to the three women before heading to the kitchen. With no catering staff, all the crew were responsible for preparing their own meals.

"That's the remaining two members of the crew here. The big, black hunk of beef was Roger Caldwell, and the short girl was Betty Harper. They're the engineers here. So now you know what we're about and you know who everyone is. Any questions?"

Claire had started jotting notes on her notepad. "You don't have any medical staff?"

"We've all received first aid training but, no, there's no doctor. There's an infirmary loaded up with some medical supplies – painkillers, plasters, bandages. I think there's a neck brace and an AED too, but no; no doctors or nurses."

"Doesn't that scare you?" asked Jazmin, wide eyed.

"No. It just makes us all very careful. Anything else?"

"What are crew sleeping arrangements? Do you work in shifts?"

Anna fished a cigarette from her pocket and lit it. "We're six people – now eight – on a rig designed to house at least ninety people. Don't worry, everyone has a room to themselves. Hell, you can have five if you want. God knows Roger spreads his stuff around a few to make a little bungalow all of his very own. To answer your other question, no, there aren't fixed shifts. I run a very loose ship here. You know why?"

"Why?" asked Jazmin.

Anna sighed out a cloud of smoke. "I trust us all to get along and do the work because we want to. If someone wants a day off, they can take one, and we all get along great for it. My only problems are when we run low on Twinkies or the *Street Fighter* machine packs in. This works for a very simple reason: no-one takes a job like this unless they *want* to work here. I think you two can settle in to this arrangement."

TWO

Jazmin followed Captain Anna and Claire into the laboratory and her eyes lit up. This was what she was hoping for when she applied for the internship. The place looked like something straight out of a movie, with microscopes, oscilloscopes, and test tubes on nearly every bench. Rock and dust samples lay in neatly labelled jars and cases. She found herself smiling without even realising it. It took a couple of seconds before she even noticed the man who was now shaking hands with and talking to Claire and Anna. She stepped forward and allowed herself to be introduced.

Bobby Kelly looked much younger than she had been expecting a scientist to look. He still had mostly black hair and was – to be honest – pretty good looking. She shook his hand, suppressing her own nervous state and remembering what she'd been told about something called "impostor syndrome". Impostor Syndrome was something that meant even those people who are generally considered to be masters in the field don't feel worthy of the attention and prestige they have. They worry they're going to be called out as impostors. As a nineteen year old intern aboard a privately owned Antarctic drilling rig and standing in an actual, honest to God laboratory...she kind of knew what they were feeling.

"Pleasure to meet you, Jazmin," Bobby said. "From what Anna was saying before you arrived, it looks like you'll be splitting your time between working with me here, and working with Kurt on the rock samples. You got any special interest?"

Jazmin shook her head. "Not especially. I'd like to try a little bit of everything while I'm here."

"That sounds good to me," said Anna. "I'll also make sure you get some drill time with Cameron, and some engineering duty with Betty and Roger. Hell, you can even do some of my paperwork if you like?"

Jazmin wasn't certain if the Captain was joking or not, so offhandedly gestured in the affirmative. "Why not?"

"What have you been working on?" Anna asked Bobby.

"Well, as you know, the drill's been out of action while Cam, Betty and Roger repair the damage..."

"What happened?" asked Claire.

"We don't know," snapped Anna, before Bobby could answer. "The drill could have hit something hard, or just struck a surface at an odd angle, making it skid a little. The tip of the drill bit is fine, but there's some scoring along its length, and the engineers wanted to check the main chuck for any stress or shock damage. We're not concerned."

"…So I've just been analysing and cataloguing the samples we've received so far," finished Bobby.

"Find anything cool?" asked Jazmin, blushing as the Captain raised an eyebrow at her.

"No, not exactly cool," smiled Bobby. "Some slate rock, a couple of nice looking plant fossils, but we haven't exactly stumbled across a live dinosaur or a mysterious forgotten city, no. To be honest, the Prospero hasn't yet hit the depth that I'd like it to. I'd like to break through the next hundred metres or so. I think we could really find something interesting then."

"Does the Prospero go that deep?" asked Claire.

"The Prospero can, theoretically, go about a mile deep, but I'm sure Cameron would rather be the one to explain all that. The reason I'd like to crack the next hundred metres is because the last few times we've attempted is when the drill has…skittered a little…resulting in the damage the Captain just described. I think there's something there we need to break through. A shell or cover of some kind, if you will."

"That's very interesting, Bobby," smiled Claire. "I look forward to seeing more of your work while I'm here."

"You'd be welcome in the lab at any time. How long are you staying for?"

"Six weeks. Myself and Jazmin here will be heading back out with the next supply 'copter."

***

Claire nudged Jazmin as they followed the Captain down several flights of metal steps, the heating whirred around them constantly, and the jangling of their footsteps seemed to echo endlessly. "He was kind of hot, wasn't he?"

"I...I didn't really notice."

"Didn't you? Oh, come on! I was expecting him to be this old, decrepit man with a massive bald spot and glasses. Are all geologists that hot?"

"Some of them, I guess."

"Am I embarrassing you?"

"What? No! I..."

Anna banged through what looked like a fire door, and they were surprised by the chill that flew around them. "The Prospero is – obviously – located at the centre of the rig, so the closer you get, the closer you get to open air and the further you get from our cosy, warm offices and bedrooms. Never, ever go directly outside without full winter gear on. If the cold doesn't kill you, the shock will make you really fucking ill. Are we absolutely clear on that?"

Jazmin mumbled a subservient reply and Claire nodded. Did "Captain" Anna think she was stupid? If it was up to her she'd spend the next six weeks hunkered around the warmest fan heater while the teenager played with her test tubes in the laboratory.

They turned down a corridor that was lined with windows. Anna gestured through them. "The Prospero."

Claire and Jazmin squinted through the blowing ice and snow at the colossal drill bit that hung in the centre of Tempest Outpost. Claire had prepared for Cameron Barnett's mad scheme to be big, but at the top, it had to be easily three hundred metres across. Serrated teeth, stained with salt and lichen stared madly back at them. It was wide, but hung two hundred metres straight down.

"I thought Bobby said that this thing could go a mile deep?"

"I'll leave that for Cameron to explain. He'll be in the control room."

Claire and Jazmin followed her through a few more corridors and fire doors, catching glimpses of the Prospero every now and again, hanging strangely like a megalithic monument in the ice, like an alien icon set in the freezing desert.

At last Anna pushed open a door into a large room full of computers and controls and levers. A dorky looking kid of about twenty years old, his thick hair slicked back with what Claire hoped was hair wax, was scrutinising some nuts and bolts through thick lensed glasses. He looked up when Anna coughed, and smiled at them warmly. "Oh, hey, Captain! These must be the new guys?"

He got awkwardly to his feet, wiping his palms on his jeans and offered handshakes to Jazmin and Claire. Claire thought he was awkward, but actually kind of endearing, although she could tell that Jazmin was less than impressed. Maybe she'd been hoping for someone hotter? Tough break, little Jazmin.

"So, what can I do for you?" asked Cameron. "You want to see the Prospero in action? I'm afraid that's probably not going to happen today. She can be a little temperamental and…well…we had an impact yesterday that kind of got us all a little worried. Due to the structure of the internal teles-"

"I filled them in on yesterday's incident, Cam," interrupted Anna. "Don't worry, we can all wait for tomorrow to see Prospero in action."

"Oh. Sure. Uh, has Bobby talked to you about wanting to push harder? He thinks that there's a shell or cover of some kind that we need to break through in order to find anything really interesting. I've sent up some of the top layer shards we picked up to him, and he thinks they're Precambrian. So that means that whatever is below the shell or shield or whatever...that's going to be old."

"*Pre*-precambrian?" said Jazmin, excitedly. "What do you mean? Hadean?"

Cameron tried to look professional and suave, and failed miserably. "Yeah. Possibly. I mean, that's more Bobby's thing. I just picked up a few terms here and there, you know. Like you do. I got one of those brains that just picks stuff up I guess. Yeah. Hadean."

Jazmin looked at him, amazed, and Claire spoke up. "So, how does the drill go down that deep? It looks to me like it's, what, two hundred metres long? That's a pretty big drill, but pretty short of a mile."

Cameron smiled. "Well, there's the part that got me the grant, and got me that nice 'Inventor of the Year' award over on the wall there. It's telescopic. I had the idea when I was seventeen, playing with a pin vice drill. You guys into *Warhammer*? Doesn't matter. The idea came quick, but getting all the moving parts to work took a couple of years, plus another two years to get the thing built. Anyway, there it is. You spin the drill, and the internal parts push out, up to a depth of about a mile. And yeah, I think we can cross our fingers for some Hadean samples tomorrow."

THREE

Anna guided Claire and Jazmin through what seemed like another hundred corridors, doors and flights of stairs, finally stopping in another cloakroom almost identical to the first they had entered off of the helipad. It was small, and wood panelled, with many winter coats hanging from bare metal hooks. Several electric fan heaters put up a feeble resistance against the Antarctic chill, and they all still shivered after having shrugged on and fastened up a heavy coat each. Anna checked that they were all wrapped up warm and had pulled up their hoods before elbowing open the door to the outside and leading them out onto the gantry.

The cold and the wind hit them like a brick wall, and it took Jazmin a moment to realise that they were on a metal walkway three hundred metres above the freezing, black sea. She stifled a scream and grabbed desperately onto the handrail. Captain Anna smiled back at her, and shouted over the wind. "Here we are! This is the closest we can get to the Prospero. Obviously Betty and Roger – the engineers – can get up directly onto the drill if they need to, but we hope that never has to happen."

The Prospero hung directly in front of them, black and jagged like a rotten tooth. Claire could see salt crusted around the sharper edges and imagined the shock generated when its colossal tip crashed into the bedrock below. It was hard to believe that this was the creation of a seventeen year old kid; then again Cameron was a pretty weird kid. Not "weird perverted" but she knew exactly what he must have been like at school. One of the outcasts. One of the geeks. And not even the cool geeks who had their own little circles full of their own little fashions and hierarchies. He had to have been one of the plain outcasts. Still, he was the one who was laughing now. She knew how much his salary was. He could have retired – quite comfortably – at the age of twenty-one after just three months working here. He had now been here for two years, arriving at the same time as construction on the Prospero had begun. Cameron wasn't in it for the money. He was in it because he wanted to be in it.

Claire felt as though she could reach out an arm and touch the colossal bit of the Prospero. When she was around things like this, she liked to reach out and touch them. It gave her a connection with things. She liked the idea that she could touch the drill, and it would spin down into the ocean bed, perhaps carrying some part of her with it. It was a sensation she had first felt in a museum, surrounded by items full of history. She had wanted to touch them all, to feel some sort of connection with the events that they had experienced. "Do you come out here often?" she asked Anna. "I mean, it's oddly beautiful."

"It's way too cold for a walk when I fancy one. Jazmin, are you okay?"

Jazmin was still gripping the handrail and hadn't budged from right outside the door. She was just staring down into the ocean.

Anna took her gently by the arm, and helped straighten her up. "Are you okay?"

"Yeah. It's just…we're really high up."

"You were higher in the helicopter. Didn't that bother you?"

"I guess I didn't really think about it. You're not going to send me home are you?"

"No, I'm not; but I think we need to get you back inside."

Anna and Claire guided the intern back into the cloakroom, sat her by a fan heater and helped her get out of her coat. Claire squatted down and looked her over. "Hey, look, if you want to get on the chopper and go back home, no one will think any the less of you. It's a hell of a thing for a girl your age to be out here."

Jazmin shook her head firmly. "I'm fine. Seriously. I guess I wasn't fully prepared for it, that's all. I assumed we were heading back onto the helipad or something. I just got surprised."

She jumped and flinched again as the door leading back into the rig banged open. Betty and Roger entered laughing and joking with each other, but fell silent when they saw the room was occupied. "Everything okay in here, Captain?" asked Roger, in a deep, warm voice.

Anna gestured dismissively. "We're fine. This is Jazmin Hayes. She's staying on as an intern for the next six weeks. This is Claire Flynn. She's a representative from Icecap who's come to make sure we're all doing a good job. You are all doing a good job, right?"

Roger laughed. "Miss Flynn, the Captain here runs a very smooth operation. Jazmin, it's a pleasure to have you on Tempest Outpost. We'll get you out there with a spanner in your hand very soon, not to worry."

Jazmin smiled, but Claire felt a little affronted – why was he on first name terms with Jazmin, and yet she remained "Miss Flynn"? It wasn't something that was worth getting wound up about, but knowing that made it even more infuriating somehow.

Betty clapped Roger on the arm and headed to the door onto the walkway. "Nice to meet you all. Roger, we got a lot to sort before we start drilling tomorrow."

"What are the issues you're having with the drill?" asked Claire.

"Nothing major. It hit something pretty hard yesterday, so we're playing it safe and checking it out for any stress damage. I don't think we'll find any, but if it's out there and we didn't find it, who knows what'll happen."

"Maintaining the Prospero's integrity is a very high priority for all of us, but especially the engineering staff," added Anna. "You know how an A-10 Warthog is basically a gun with the plane built around it? Well, the Tempest Outpost is a massive drill with a rig built around it. If the Prospero were badly damaged enough, then this whole station could be structurally compromised."

"That's right," said Roger. "If the Prospero collapsed – and I'm not saying that it ever could or would – then there's every chance the whole rig would collapse. That's why Icecap Industries keeps such a skeleton staff aboard, and why it pays us so handsomely for our place here."

Claire's glance flickered to Jazmin and wondered how little – if at all – the intern was being paid to work here. When she was a student, any work experience was always unpaid, although you might get travel compensation if you were lucky. She at least hoped that the ride in the Black Hawk had been complimentary. She shuddered to think how much that would cost.

Betty scratched at her hair and lit a cigarette. "Anyway, we'll see you lovely ladies later. Kurt was making noises about cooking dinner for everyone – a nice welcome party for the new members of the crew."

With a wave, Roger followed her out and onto the gantry. Claire looked back to Jazmin. "Are you okay now?"

"Yes, I'm fine."

"Captain, I think we'd like to be shown to our quarters now, if that's okay with you. It's been a long day travelling, and we're both exhausted."

"Of course. This way."

***

Anna gestured them into their rooms, which were much larger than they had been expecting. There was a bed, a desk with a PC, a television and what hotels referred to as "Tea and Coffee Making Facilities".

"You two are just across the corridor from each other. If you need more space, I'm happy to unlock a couple more rooms for you. As I mentioned before, we're not exactly crowded in here and Roger's place takes up five rooms. One just for his decks and vinyl. Feel free to shout at him if he gets too loud, but truth be told he plays pretty good stuff most of the time."

Claire looked around the room, trying to hide how impressed she was. "Looks great. I can't wait to move in."

"The TVs work?" asked Jazmin. "I didn't think you'd get broadcasts down here."

"We get digital signals, and Icecap are kind enough to fork out for the movie and sport packages for us. If the weather's bad we lose it, though. In that case there is a database online that's kind of a Netflix type thing."

"Wow."

"Hey, you're here to work. You can catch up with *Pretty Little Liars* in your downtime."

"Of course, Captain."

"Come on, let's go get your luggage from the Black Hawk."

FOUR

Jazmin had a mixture of feelings as she watched the Black Hawk's rotor start to spin; feelings that only intensified once the helicopter was up in the air and sailing away from Tempest Outpost. The Captain had told her to take twelve hours off to recover from the flight and maybe get over a little of her jet lag, and while the offer was appreciated, it really didn't help with her conflicted feelings. She was excited and full of adrenaline, which meant that she really wanted to get to work straight away, no matter what that "work" might actually entail.

Yet, she was also exhausted, and – truth be told – pretty scared. It felt like her first day of University when her mum and dad had dropped her off at the halls of residence before a tearful goodbye. She had sat in her room and wondered if she'd made the right decision. She worried about her family, and wondered if they'd be okay. Of course, if she needed to get home it would only have been six hours or so on the train. Out here off the coast of Antarctica would be rather a longer commute. And the "trains" only ran every six weeks unless there was an emergency.

Captain Anna had gone back to her office, Claire had gone to her own quarters, so Jazmin went to the canteen to see if there was anything to snack on. Or anyone to talk to.

She pushed open the doors into the cavernous interior – a reminder that the rig was built for a staff many times its actual complement – and found Cameron sat at a table, eating a sandwich and reading on a Kindle. She waved "hi" to him, though he didn't seem to notice. She grabbed a bag of Doritos, an apple and a bottle of water from the canteen, sat across from him and tried again. "What are you reading?"

"Oh, uh…hi…it's Stephen King's *The Gunslinger*. I heard they were doing a movie of it, and it's always been on my pile of ones to read when I can get the chance. Have you read it?"

"A long time ago. I remember thinking it was okay but I prefer his horror stuff. What do you think?"

"I'm not even halfway through yet. So…what do you think of Tempest Outpost?"

"It's…pretty big."

Cameron laughed and opened a can of Coke Zero. "Yeah. It feels like a ghost town, or something out of *The Walking Dead* sometimes. I've been here longer than any of the others. I think I was one of the first on here after it was built, actually. Haven't been home in a long time."

"How long do the rest of the crew work?"

"They're on a rota. It works out something roughly like twelve weeks on and six weeks off, or something like that. It's nice when Anna's in charge because she's pretty laid back. Better than Fred. He's a bit grouchy."

"Anna seems nice," said Jazmin, with a yawn. "So, if you don't work those shifts, what is yours?"

"I haven't been off the rig in…ten months now? I went home for Christmas. I think everyone did. Overwintering here isn't a lot of fun, you know."

"I can imagine. The cold's actually kind of terrifying out on the pad, or on the gantry."

"Yeah, I know. It takes some getting used to, and even then I try and stay inside as much as I can. I recommend you do the same."

The conversation trailed off. Cameron filled the awkward silence. "Look, everyone here is quite a bit older than us – I mean, maybe not that Claire girl, she's only, what, twenty-five? But if you want, you can always hang out in my rooms?"

Jazmin couldn't stop her eyebrow from raising.

"Oh! No, not like that! It's just I've got a PS4 and an Xbox down there, plus I've got a Blu-ray player hooked up and a bunch of movies, so I'm not limited by the mainstream choices Icecap beams in here. I just thought…well, the invite's there."

Jazmin smiled. "Sure. I might take you up on that."

"Cool. Anyway, I should be heading back to the control room. We're drilling tomorrow, so I should check that everything's in order."

"Of course. I'm going to head to bed for a bit, anyway. I've been awake for about twenty hours now, and it's been a hell of a day."

"Sure. I'll see you tomorrow."

***

The following morning, Jazmin was woken by a sharp banging on her door. Rubbing sleep from her eyes, it took her a second to remember where she was – worried for a moment that she'd gotten too drunk at the student union again, and woken up in some stranger's bed. She hobbled over to the door, still wrapped in a duvet, and opened it up. "Captain" Anna Morris was there, beaming at her. "Good morning."

"What time is it?"

"It's seven in the morning."

"Okay. Uh…shit. Was I supposed to do something?"

"No, not at all. Consider this your friendly wake up call. Get washed and dressed then come meet me in my office. If you get the chance, do you think that you could swing by the canteen and grab me a coffee and a couple of Twinkies?"

Jazmin wasn't sure she'd be able to find her way around unassisted yet. The stairs and corridors of Tempest Outpost could only really be described as "labyrinthine". "Uh…I guess."

Anna laughed. "Okay, forget the coffee. Head to the Prospero's control room in an hour. You can manage that, right? It's where you met Cameron."

"Yes. I can find it."

***

When Jazmin arrived, Anna, Claire and Cameron were watching the Prospero revolving gently, as though it were limbering up like a gymnast. Anna tapped her cigarette into a foil ashtray, and rested a hand on Cameron's shoulder. "Think it'll break through this time?"

Cameron smiled. "Yes, Ma'am. I think it could have done so yesterday, it was just Roger and Betty weren't so convinced."

"Do you have any idea what it was that the drill struck to cause such a shock?"

"No," murmured Cameron, clicking some switches. "I still got nothing. I was reading up on the geology of the area all last night, and there's nothing that can account for it."

Jazmin clicked the door shut quietly behind her. "Could it be something man-made? Like a shipwreck or something?"

Anna shook her head. "This isn't exactly a shipping route. A wooden ship would have rotted to nothing by now – or at least provide no resistance to the Prospero."

Cameron interrupted. "Oh, please. The *Bismarck* wouldn't provide any resistance to the Prospero."

"No-one's insulting your girlfriend, Cameron," said Anna, punctuating it with a playful slap to the back of the head.

Jazmin stepped closer to them. "Is there anything I should be doing? I mean…what would you like done?"

"Just watch and learn," smiled Anna. "This is pretty much the heart of what we're here to do."

Cameron adjusted a dial and threw a lever on the control panel in front of him, and the drill kicked up a gear, spinning faster and obviously more powerfully. A grin lit up his face and Anna knew that this was the highlight of the job for him. Truth to be told, it was for her as well. There were days - sometimes weeks - of downtime, and this was the only real excitement there was between supply drops. Another switch was thrown and the drill began to telescope down.

Anna noticed that Jazmin's jaw was wide open. "Pretty impressive the first time, isn't it?"

"It's amazing," whispered Jazmin, turning to Cameron. "You really designed that all by yourself?"

Cameron was too immersed in his work to turn away from the drill and the control panel. "I'm not just a pretty face, m'lady."

Anna cuffed him again. "I've told you to stop calling women 'm'lady'. It makes you sound creepy."

"Sorry, m'lady."

Cameron threw another three switches in rapid succession and Anna held her breath as the Prospero span, telescoped and crashed down into the water below. They were two or three hundred metres above the ocean, but the drill went with such a crash that droplets of water still spattered across the window in front of them. "Well, we've reached the water…" she whispered.

The rig shuddered and vibrated slightly, and Anna felt Jazmin catch onto her arm for support. "It's okay. That's pretty normal," she said, noting that Jazmin hadn't moved her hand away yet.

"Approaching bedrock in five…four…"

Anna held her breath, her cigarette ash growing long.

"Three...two..."

There was a screeching sound that caused her and Jazmin to slap their hands over their ears.

"Okay, I misjudged it a little," muttered Cameron. "We're at bedrock and...we're through."

"We're through?" squealed Jazmin. "Really?"

"Of course we are. The Prospero was designed by a genius, you know."

"So, what happens next?"

FIVE

Betty and Roger watched the drill descend from the gantry where Jazmin had had her panic attack the day before. Betty sparked up a joint and watched the colossal drill spin and extend downwards. "Reckon it'll make it through this time?"

Roger pulled a face. "I expect so. I mean, what can be down there that something that size can't smash through?"

"Ice. Alien spacecraft. An alien spacecraft buried in the ice."

"That one of your stupid sci-fi references?"

"Of course not."

Roger chuckled. "You know you're just as big a nerd as Cameron. Surprised the two of you haven't started up a little *Dungeons and Dragons* club."

"If we found something buried in the ice, we'd all just have to mark its perimeter and then it'd slowly dawn on us all that we were standing around a flying saucer."

"Do you watch any normal movies?"

Betty took a drag of her joint and replied in a tight, high voice as she held her breath. "You mean movies about carjacking and street racing and shit like that? Yeah, sure. So long as there's monsters in them."

Roger laughed a deep laugh. "Watching horror movies out here would freak me out. You ever see that one where they're out in the arctic and one of the dogs turns out to be a monster and then it turns out the monster can just look like whatever it wants to look like, so they're not sure who's a monster and who's human?"

"I might have seen it once or twice, yeah."

"Man, I could not watch that out here. I'd never sleep until the chopper came to take me home."

"It's a good movie," Betty said, passing the joint to Roger, who took a drag. The Prospero splashed into the water beneath them, and she suppressed a shiver. "You ever stop to think about what's actually down there? I mean, it could be anything. They say that under the sea is like…just…an alien world. We know very little about it. I mean, you know somewhere like the Mariana Trench…"

"The what?"

"The Mariana Trench. Imagine the Grand Canyon under the sea and you're almost there. You could put Mount Everest in it and Everest wouldn't show above the surface of the water. It's insanely deep. Do you ever think about the kind of shit that could be living and growing down there? Hell, there could be an entire race of people down there that we'll never see."

Roger shivered. "Knock it off, man, you're freaking me out. I'm now expecting that we're going to see the Kraken or some shit coming up from the ocean."

Betty coughed a laugh, watching the Prospero begin drilling into the water. "Chill out, man. All we're going to find out here is fossils. Maybe some oil. That's it."

***

Another shudder ran through the control room, and several notifications popped up on Cameron's computer screens. Jazmin hurried over, and peered over his shoulder. "What's happening?"

"The Prospero's broken through the obstacle we hit yesterday. Just…smashed through it like it's an egg-shell. It…it seems like it's hollow inside."

"Hollow?"

"Yeah. Must be, like, a geode or something."

"What's a geode?" asked Claire, aware she was asking a dumb question in a room of geologists.

"You ever see those hollow rocks that have been cut open, showing a load of tiny little crystal stalactites and stalagmites inside?" asked Anna. "You usually get them in shitty gift shops or in those places that sell Tarot cards and vegetarian cookbooks."

"Yeah."

"Those are geodes. It happens when gas bubbles form in volcanic rocks. Put simply."

"I got you. So the Prospero just found a giant one?"

Cameron was hurriedly scrolling and clicking through a load of windows and graphs on his computer screen. "Yeah, or an egg or a cyst or an abscess, depending on how gross you want to be. I'm going to begin excavation, see what we can bring up to study."

"You can do that?" asked Jazmin, a little amazed.

"Yeah, I mean, there'd be no point in just smashing about in the ocean if we couldn't bring anything up to study, right? I'll bring up some samples, then Kurt and Bobby will pore through them in the lab. I'll be there too, of course. Uh, you can come hang out too, if you like? I mean, if it's all right with the Captain."

Anna smiled. "Just make sure she's home by eleven. It's a school night."

Cameron blushed and Jazmin laughed. She squeezed his shoulder gently to let him know not to be flustered by it, and he turned back to his work. He navigated through various windows, charts and diagrams at speed, finishing with adjusting some physical dials and switches on the console in front of him. "Okay. The excavator is bringing stuff up now."

"Where does it dump whatever it brings up?" asked Claire.

Cameron was too occupied with the computer to answer, so Anna spoke up. "An internal chamber inside the drill carries rock samples up the entire length of the shaft. Once it's there, we can unbolt a compartment and just pick up whatever we need, and then dump the rest of it."

"What do you think it was that we broke through?" asked Jazmin.

"Ice. A layer of sediment. It's too early to say. It's rather dark down there, too, you know."

"You think it could be Hadean rock down there?"

Cameron clicked a final checkbox on the computer and the drill ground to a stop before spinning in the reverse direction and telescoping back in on itself. "Well, we got samples. They'll be ready for Kurt and Bobby to analyse in about twenty minutes. I'll head down to the lab, too. Anyone else want to come?"

Jazmin smiled. "You know I do."

Anna's eyes remained locked on the Prospero as it spun back into its home position. "What's that?"

"What's what?" asked Cameron.

"There. On the tip section."

A white, claggy compound was smeared across the tip of the drill. It looked like the teeth had gotten a bad case of plaque, as if it had spun into a massive lump of discarded chewing gum at the bottom of the ocean. Anna felt her arm hairs rise, though she didn't know why.

Cameron stood up to peer closer through the window. "I don't know. It could be…some kind of chalk, maybe?"

"It looks too viscous to be chalk. It looks like…goopy resin."

Cameron shrugged. "Whatever it is, it'll need to be cleaned off before we try another excavation. Get Betty and Roger on it please, Captain."

"I will. I'm going back to my office. I need to make a log of all this, because sure as shit no-one else ever bothers. Miss Flynn, you want to accompany me, or do you want to go to the lab?"

"You can call me Claire; and I'll come with you. I have to see how your administration systems work if I'm going to be able to do a full report."

"You sure? Don't want to go and look at wet rocks instead?"

"I'm sure. Your office is warm and has coffee."

"That it does. And Twinkies. Jazmin, why don't you help out the boys in the lab today? We can get you on paperwork when things are a little more boring around here."

"Sounds good to me, Captain."

***

Cameron and Jaz were waiting in the laboratory when Kurt and Bobby arrived with the samples the Prospero had brought up. Kurt placed the large tray full of dust and rocks in front of them. "As you can see, it's a pretty weird haul."

The tray was full of wet sand, shellfish fragments, several chips of slate and four strange looking rocks. They were all roughly spherical and about the size of a grapefruit. An odd crystalline sheen covered their otherwise dull, brown surface; although this could just have been the laboratory lights reflecting on their dull surface. Cameron reached down and picked one up, tapping it with the knuckle of his right hand. "Geodes?"

Jazmin felt a strange gooseflesh. It was surely a coincidence, but it felt strange that they had been talking about geodes not moments before. "Is it normal to find that many so close together?"

***

Betty and Roger looked up at the white gunk embedded in the teeth of the drill. It had dried and hardened slightly so that it now just looked like chalk; or, Betty reflected, bird shit. "Fire hose should shift most of it. I hope it doesn't come down to climbing out there with a scrubbing brush."

"What do you suppose it is?" asked Roger.

"Chalk, I reckon. Or something goopy they hit down there. I'm sure it's pretty normal, whatever it is."

"You ever see *Alien*?"

"I think I might have seen it once or twice, yeah."

"There were two engineers like us in that, right?"

"Right."

SIX

Cameron picked up one of the geodes and shook it gently. "Something's rattling in there."

Bobby shrugged. "Maybe some crystals broke loose or something."

Cameron pulled a face. "I dunno. It feels more…substantial than that."

Jazmin reached down and picked up another. "Wow, it's cold."

Cameron smiled. "What did you expect? It's been at the bottom of the ocean around the Antarctic since…well…how long do we think? Can we carbon date it?"

"Of course, we can," said Kurt, almost offended. "I'll just take a sample."

"How long does carbon dating take?" asked Jazmin, wide-eyed, still feeling a little bit like this was all a dream, or happening to someone else. She felt like Dorothy, caught in a hurricane. "I mean, when we did it at college, it took a couple of days, but we had to send it off to another lab in Arkansas or somewhere. So, what do we do?"

Kurt had taken a small chip from one of the geodes, and scurried off with it and Bobby to the other side of the laboratory. "Probably two or three minutes," he called over his shoulder. "We're a little more high tech – and not to mention better situated – than Arkansas University."

"I've never heard us called 'better situated' before," muttered Bobby.

Cameron was prodding through the sand and shellfish fragments with his pen. "There's a few leg segments and stuff here. Probably just dead matter from the surface of...whatever it was we punched through. Ice, I guess. There's none of it here."

Jazmin pulled a face. "It's still smeared all over the drill. Could you get a sample from there?"

"You want to try climbing out there to get some?" asked Cameron, distractedly. "If it's not ice, then it's just chalk or sediment. It's not a big deal; and even if it is, we can just scoop down and get some more, right?"

"Sure. You're the boss."

"Anna's the boss. I just *should be* the boss."

"I guess so," replied Jazmin, a little surprised by the venom in his voice.

"Any guesses before the final results are announced?" called Bobby from the other side of the room.

"Precambrian?" Cameron guessed.

"I'm gonna push the boat out and say Hadean," said Jazmin, flashing a smile at Cameron.

"You really think they could be Hadean?"

"Well, we're out here on the frontier, aren't we? Anything's possible."

Kurt walked very slowly across the laboratory to them, never taking his eyes off of the small print out in his hands.

"Come on!" called Bobby. "Don't keep us in suspense. What is it?"

Kurt shook his head. "I…something must have been corrupted. Or contaminated. Whatever. I need to take another sample."

"Oh. Sure," said Cameron, who had picked up another of the geodes and was studying it in his hand. "I'm going to crack this one open. Anyone object?"

"I do!" shouted Kurt. "These have been down there for…for a very long time. Who knows what's inside? It could be toxic gas for all we know. Just…give me a moment. Let's do the carbon dating first. Then we can…we can take an x-ray or something. Just, please, be patient. As Jazmin said, we are on the frontier here. What's an extra fifteen minutes caution?"

Cameron was rattled by the outburst from the normally super calm geologist, and placed the geode back in the sample tray. "All right, Kurt. Anything you say."

Jazmin sidled up to him. "Is he okay?"

"I don't know. I've never seen him this on edge before. It's like…super weird."

The laboratory fell silent as Kurt carried out a second carbon dating test. The only sound was the whirring of the heating, and then the gentle buzz as the carbon dating machine printed out its results. Kurt snatched it and studied it intensely before slumping down into a chair. "My god."

The others rushed over to him. Jazmin went to check Kurt was okay, while Bobby and Cameron snatched at the print out.

"Four point five six billion years old!" yelled Bobby.

"That's insane. The Earth itself is only 4.56 billion years old," said Cameron.

"Yes. This rock is from when the earth was still a molten mass," said Kurt. "They shouldn't be. I mean, they can't be. Everything was just…molten. There's just no way that a geode could have formed. It makes no sense. No sense at all."

Jazmin was stunned. "So they're not Hadean. They're…"

"Chaotian!" finished Cameron. "Yes. The first era, from before the Earth's surface had even cooled. You all realise what a massive discovery this is, right?"

"I realise," Kurt muttered. "I just…don't know what it means."

The room fell into silence for a few moments as they all contemplated the significance of this discovery. If these geodes, these igneous rocks really were the age of the planet, it could change everything that mankind understood of its geology.

Cameron was the first to break the silence. "I want to X-ray one. See what we're dealing with."

Kurt nodded, picking up a different geode from the one he had carbon dated, and Jazmin noticed that his hand was still shaking a little. "Sure. I mean…we could. We should, right?"

Bobby and Cameron exchanged a look. They had never seen Kurt rattled by anything before. Seeing him like this was downright disconcerting. They both knew that they had stumbled across something big, but Kurt seemed to literally be in shock.

"I, uh, can do that if you like, Kurt. Why don't you take a break?" asked Bobby.

"No, no. I'm fine. Sorry."

Kurt placed the geode into the X-ray machine, and prepared the photography equipment. The room had once again fallen silent, magnifying every sound he made.

"This is a hell of a first day," Jazmin's voice came out in a hoarse whisper and she cleared her throat before continuing. "Everyone else on my course is probably cleaning test tubes or filing receipts for petri dishes. Here I am, on an experimental drilling rig, and it looks like we just turned our knowledge of geology on its head."

Cameron chuckled, and Bobby punched her playfully on the arm. "You must be our good luck charm. To be honest, it had all been pretty dull until you showed up."

A buzzer sounded, and a small orange LED lit up indicating that the X-Ray was processed, and the resulting image was ready. Kurt took it, nervously rubbing his beard with the other hand, and clipped it up to the light box so that everyone could see.

"That's a fucked up looking geode," said Cameron.

They had all expected to see that the potato sized rock was mostly hollow, with the inside of the "skin" covered in small, crystalline formations. Jazmin had seen a hundred geodes in her time, in museums, laboratories, gift shops...she knew exactly what was supposed to be there. What was actually inside looked like something from a horror movie. "Is that a...?"

Bobby squinted up closer to the lightbox. "It's a weird mineral formation. It looks like...well, it looks like a tarantula."

Jazmin felt her arm hairs rise as she saw what the lab assistant was looking at. She could make out what looked like legs, although if it were a tarantula, it was pretty squashed up in its little cocoon.

Bobby gestured across the X-ray with his pen. "Abdomen, thorax, legs..."

"Pareidolia," said Cameron. "Your brain is finding meaning in random patterns; it's no different to seeing faces in the clouds."

"I see it, too," said Jazmin. "It looks like a spider."

"Oh, come on. Let's crack the damn thing open, then. It'll just be a weird igneous rock and, well, it's probably not even Hadean. I mean, I don't know what it'll be, but to find a rock that's theoretically possibly older than the planet is enough for me."

Bobby turned to Kurt. "Do you want to crack it open? It's your laboratory, so we'll go with what you say."

"I think we should."

Cameron grabbed disposable gas masks for them all, and they soon surrounded the selected geode. Kurt steadied it and the chisel in one hand, holding a mallet in the other. "Ready?"

"Ready," whispered Jazmin.

The hammer gently tapped down four or five times before the outer shell of the geode cracked neatly around the circumference. Kurt slowly prised the two halves apart. A shimmer of crystal around the inside of the shell showed that it was a geode of some kind, but this was not what any of them noticed first.

There was no dead space inside the geode, where gas had once been. Instead, out tumbled a lump that was definitely and undeniably a cramped, fossilised spider.

Cameron excitedly picked it up, not even stopping to pull on latex gloves. "Look at that! That's…it's a fucking spider!"

Jazmin felt her stomach turn. She wasn't good with spiders at the best of times. Antediluvian ones were a whole other ball game. "But…spiders didn't evolve until the early Cretaceous. And those are spiders. Tarantulas like this one didn't come along until…"

"Tarantulas have been found in the Triassic," interrupted Kurt. "But, this rock is at least Hadean. And if this all tallies up, this will change everything we know about the evolution of life on this planet."

SEVEN

At the end of a long day in the laboratory, and despite Jazmin's gentle deterring, Cameron insisted on walking her back to her room. He also kept mentioning that they could go back to his rooms if they didn't feel like sleeping, which Jazmin found more than a little grating after the third time. She said, truthfully, that she was dog tired, and would see him in the morning. She was terrified that he was going to try and lean in for a kiss at her doorway, but he didn't. She couldn't quite work out if he actually *liked her* liked her, or if he was just a dork and completely awkward around girls.

She wanted to call her mother in London, but it was seven in the evening on the rig, which meant it would be six in the morning with her. A little early for a social call. She decided to take a quick nap, and then call her and go get something to eat, but as soon as her head hit the pillow, the jet lag and the excitement of the day knocked her out like a punch.

***

Cameron retired to his room, and burnt his way through a four pack of coke and a few hours playing on his PlayStation before finally crashing out for the evening, his head filled with questions as to what the day's discoveries – if they were true – would mean. The other three geodes had all been X-rayed, and they too, contained what looked like spiders. One, maybe two, could be chalked up to pareidolia – the scientific term for seeing faces in clouds and tree bark – but not four. Something momentous had occurred in Tempest Outpost's Laboratory, and he couldn't believe he was lucky enough to have seen it.

***

Roger and Betty didn't go to bed that night. Instead, between the movie services and Betty's stash of DVDs, they had a movie night in her rooms, with Roger being introduced to all sort of horror movies he'd never seen before: *The Gate*, *Mimic* and *Them!*, which was a particular favourite of Betty's.

"I had a copy I taped off the TV when I was a kid," she told him. "I went through a phase of watching it every day for a whole summer. I've probably seen it more than I've seen any other."

"Yeah, I think every kid goes through that with a movie. Mine was *Return of the Jedi*."

"Every kid loves *Star Wars*. Every adult, too."

***

Anna and Claire shut down their offices at around six in the evening, and grabbed a microwave dinner together. It turned out to be pretty unimpressive, but that was not a surprise.

"How are things with Stephen?" asked Anna. "You two had just moved in together last time I saw you."

"Oh, Steve? Yeah, things are really good."

"How's he coping with six weeks without you?"

"I imagine he'll be filling it with Xbox, pizza and football. How about you? Are you seeing anyone?"

Anna stirred her cottage pie around on her plate. "Not really. The shifts I pull here make it hard to make long relationships work."

"You never been tempted to hook up with some of the crew here?"

"Tempted, sure. But I'd never act on it. It'd just make things too awkward. You want to have a massive bust up with a boyfriend, and still have to live in the middle of fucking nowhere together for another six months?"

"Yeah, that'd be awkward as hell; especially as you'd be their boss. I think Cameron is sweet on Jazmin."

"She's cute, and he's probably still a virgin. He's tried it on with every girl we've ever had aboard, myself included."

"Really?"

"Yeah. It's nice to have the attention, but...no way. Not enough beer in the world."

Claire laughed. "It's good to see you again. I really wish we could make this happen more often, you know?"

"Yeah. Me too."

They then went back to their own rooms, read for a while, and both fell asleep around the same time. Claire set an alarm for six o'clock in the morning, and Captain Anna didn't bother, because work started when she decided it started – that was a perk of the job she was most grateful for.

***

Kurt and Bobby were the last to stop work for the day, having sealed all of the geodes in small, plastic containers with pop on lids, like the kind pet shops sold crickets and locusts in. It had been a long day and their feet ached and their eyes stung.

"Any final conclusions?" asked Bobby, pulling the door closed.

"No. Nothing final. We broke geology, Bobby. If what we've discovered all rings true, then that throws everything out. Prehistory may as well go back to the drawing board. Invertebrate life forms at a time when the planet hadn't even finished cooling? What the hell does that mean? How did they survive? No life could survive at that temperature…"

"And four of them all together?"

"Oh, come on, Bobby. We only found four. There could be hundreds of them down there. Thousands. There could be spiders, millipedes, cockroaches, unicycling dachshunds for all we know. It just…God damn it, it doesn't make any sense."

"In a way it has to."

Kurt was confused. "What do you mean?"

"Well, if it's proven to be true, then it has to make sense. The rest of knowledge will have to fall in line with what we've discovered here today. The rest of the world will make sense around what we've discovered."

"Yes. Yes, I suppose it will. Strange to think, isn't it?"

Bobby clapped him on the arm, and they headed to their rooms. "Don't worry. It's not going to affect the price of a pint, is it? It's just old rocks."

***

The geodes sat in the darkness of the laboratory as – around them – Tempest Outpost drifted off to sleep. The extracted spider lay in its plastic container, on a shelf, padded with a little kitchen towel. It had spent untold millennia at the bottom of the coldest body of water known to humanity, imprisoned in its cocoon within a cocoon. Now, it was feeling warmth for the first time in an eternity. The two fan heaters were running twenty-four hours a day to maintain the laboratory at a comfortable room temperature. Compared to four billion years at the bottom of the Antarctic Ocean, it was a veritable sauna.

The spider felt the warmth permeate its exoskeleton and its forelegs began to uncurl and stretch, the joints clicking as the chitin worked out its cramp. Its pedipalps twitched, and its teeth stretched out. At this, it was exhausted, and was forced to rest for an hour or so. Finally, it felt some primal instinct motivating it to movement. With a series of snapping pops, the spider stretched out its full, six-inch leg span, and began to patrol the borders of its cage.

It didn't take the thing long to work out that the roof was incredibly flimsy and, with a few hard nudges of its abdomen, the lid popped off and onto the foot with a tiny clatter. The spider, now exhausted again, rested, gently twitching its pedipalps and spinnerets.

At firstly awkwardly, but with growing ease and rapidity, the spider crawled up and over the side of its container, and scuttled along the shelf, sensing the nearness of the other geodes. Reaching the next in line, it squashed itself against the wall behind it, and then stretched out its legs. The container slid forward on the shelf before dropping the five feet to the floor. The lid popped open and the geode rolled out, striking the leg of a desk, and cracking neatly down the middle. The first spider crept to the edge of the shelf and watched as two legs, then four, unfolded steadily from the cracked geode and the new spider emerged from its chrysalis.

The second spider embraced the warmth in the room rapidly, and scurried upto the first spider. Pedipalps and teeth twitched as if in some bizarre sign language, and the two of them worked together to quickly free the others.

The four impossibly old spiders searched for a means of escape, and – finding no windows, and the only door too heavy for them to move – stopped to rest once more. The second spider – the largest of them so far – concentrated on its surroundings, and noticed that a current of air was coming from a vent high up in the wall behind the shelving. Leading its three compatriots, the lead spider climbed up the shelving unit, leaving a trail of webbing for its weaker and smaller brothers and sisters to follow.

The grill covering the airflow stymied the tarantula for a moment, but its powerful jaws made short work of the cheap metal, bending and stretching a hole large enough for them all to squeeze through.

As the crew of Tempest Outpost slept, the four spiders crawled down the air ducting in search of somewhere warm to hide up for the night, while their strength returned.

EIGHT

Bobby was the first to enter the laboratory the following morning. With his coffee in one hand, he used the other to unlock the door and shove it clumsily open with his shoulder. Stopping to wipe his stinging eyes, he fumbled on the light switch. As the strip lighting flickered into life, he instantly knew that something was up. When he noticed the shattered rocks and containers on the floor he felt sick to his stomach. Had one of the shelves collapsed? No, they were all still there, and all structurally sound. He dropped to his knees on the floor, and squinted under the desks and machines. The fragments of the geode shells were still there, but the spiders were gone.

Adrenaline flooded through him, and he dashed to the intercom. He hurriedly keyed in the code for Cameron's room, and it buzzed for a few seconds before being answered. "It's seven in the morning, dudes."

"Cam, it's Bobby. Can you come to the laboratory, like, right away? Shit is fucked up and I need you. I'm going to call Kurt, too, okay?"

"Uh, sure, man. What's happened? Are the spiders okay?"

"They're gone."

"What? What the hell do you mean 'gone'?"

"They've busted out. They've escaped. They've just disappeared. Get the fuck up here, man."

"Okay. I'll be there in a couple of minutes."

***

In less than five minutes, both Kurt and Cameron had joined Bobby in the laboratory. "This is just insane," whispered Kurt. "Fossils don't get up and walk away."

Cameron could feel his gooseflesh rising. "Maybe they weren't fossils, Kurt. Maybe they were just...hibernating."

"You seriously believe that?"

"Kurt, what we learned yesterday turned everything on its head. If these things are alive and running around this room somewhere, then that seems a perfectly reasonable hypothesis to me. At this point I wouldn't blink an eyelid if they had strutted across the floor singing Dolly Parton hits."

"It doesn't make sense."

"We have evidence. You need to get your head around that."

Kurt hesitated for a moment, before putting his hands up in surrender and sinking into a chair. "So, what do we do? Just go hunting for them with a tumbler and a coaster?"

Bobby had grabbed a couple of empty storage tubs. "Pretty much. When I was at college one of my housemates had a tarantula that escaped. What she did was to make sure that every room had a Tupperware container in it, so that if you saw it, you had to trap it under it."

Cameron suppressed a shiver. "Man, that'd have killed me. Did you find it?"

"Yeah, I caught it. I was having a shower when I saw it up on the ceiling. I managed to coax it into the Tupperware and left it for her to take care of when she got home."

"Jesus. I don't know I could have done that."

Bobby handed him one of the plastic containers. "Well, I guess we're going to find out. Come on, guys, they've got to be in this room somewhere."

"How many do you think we're dealing with?" asked Kurt.

"All four geodes are smashed…hatched…so I think it's safe to assume we're looking for four."

"Or one big, fat one," suggested Cameron.

The room fell silent as the three men began their search. Bobby mentioned that they didn't know if the spiders were terrestrial or arboreal, and so would have to search both low and high. He squatted to check the floors, Kurt – as the tallest among them – checked the ceilings, and Cameron took it upon himself to search the shelving that the spiders had originally been stored on. He reasoned that they could just be squatting behind any of the containers on the shelving, waiting for prey, or perhaps to molt after their long hibernation.

One by one, he pulled the containers out, expecting at any moment to be treated to the scurrying of long legs moving further into the darkness or – much worse – the flash of teeth and a hideous screeching, hissing sound. With the bottom two shelves cleared, he stood up to stretch and take a breather. As he leaned backwards, easing out his aching spine, his eyes fell upon the ventilation grill near the ceiling. He felt cold adrenaline flood his body as he saw the way the bars had been bent out of shape into a tarantula sized tunnel.

"Fuck."

***

The entire crew sat around a fold-out dining table in the canteen, listening to Kurt, Bobby and Cameron relate the news of their discovery, and also of its escape. Captain Anna leaned her head in her hands and groaned loudly. "I did not sign up for this shit."

Jazmin played with her fingers nervously, not sure what to say. Claire shivered. "I hate spiders."

Anna thumped the table noisily with her fist. "Why the fuck didn't you guys tell me this sooner?"

"In fairness Captain, until this morning there was nothing to report," offered Jazmin.

"Nothing to report? You don't talk. You're a fucking work experience kid. Kurt, why the fuck didn't you tell me sooner?"

Kurt shrugged. "It's as Jazmin says – there was nothing to report. You knew we were analysing the rock samples that the Prospero had brought up, and that's exactly what we had been doing. We were acting under the belief that the…invertebrates we'd discovered were fossils. The Prospero has dredged up fossils before and, frankly, you were never that interested in them."

Bobby cut in. "Captain, these fossils were such an unexpected discovery that we wanted to be doubly sure that they were what we thought they were. At the stage we left them last night, we still weren't sure. Now, we know that they're…well…something else."

"Ain't that the truth," muttered Roger, lighting a cigarette.

"So, what do we do now?" asked Anna.

The room fell silent. Claire was the one to break the silence. "Well, we have to catch those things, right? I'm not going to sleep well at night knowing that a dinosaur tarantula could be creeping into my bed. If you didn't sign up for this, Anna, imagine how I feel."

Anna rubbed her eyes. "Okay, but how in the hell do we go about finding four tarantula sized creatures in a fucking drilling rig? Do you guys have any idea how many ducts and cables and crawlspaces and bolt holes there are aboard this thing? A needle in a haystack would be a piece of piss in comparison."

"There is an alternative," suggested Cameron.

"I'm all ears."

"Bobby, how long did it take you to find your housemate's missing tarantula?"

"I don't know. I don't think it was more than a day or two. She said if they didn't find it by the end of the week it'd probably be dead anyway."

"Right. So, it's reasonable to suppose that these things will similarly suffer in a foreign environment. Two, maybe three days, and these things will just be desiccating in an air duct somewhere. Or in Claire's bed."

"Not funny."

"It was a little bit funny."

Jazmin shook her head. "That doesn't hold up. We don't know anything about these spiders. For all we know this is the ideal environment for them. They could positively thrive."

Anna nodded. "Jazmin's right. We've got to at least try to find them. If we can't find them in a week, I'll be happy to call off the search, but I want us at least trying. For the moment though, I want radio silence on this. I don't need Icecap knowing that we made and then lost a scientific discovery. I'm not talking to them until I've got good news to share. You with me?"

The crew murmured their assent. "Okay. For today, everyone go with your gut and just go looking. We'll draw up a more detailed plan tomorrow if we need to. Anything else?"

"Yes, Captain," said Cameron. "I'm pretty sure that these things will be dead in a day or two. Frankly, I consider searching for them to be a total waste of time and resources. I'd like to just write these ones off and fire up the Prospero again. We'll pick up some more geodes – or eggs, or cocoons, or whatever they are – and this time we can be much more careful with them. We'll keep them in locked boxes to prevent escape."

"No way. Uh-uh," cut in Claire. "You want to bring in more dinospiders, while these ones are still skittering and scuttling around? Fuck that. You want to do that, you can wait until I'm back home."

"I'm with Claire," said Betty. "We fix one problem before compounding it."

"You're outvoted and overruled, Cam," said Anna, pulling on an Icecap Industries baseball cap. "We fix these bugs first. Let's get to it. Claire, you can hide on your own, or you can search with someone. Your choice."

"Fine. I'll come with."

NINE

Bobby and Kurt, perhaps somewhat obviously, took it upon themselves to investigate the laboratory, along with its surrounding rooms and corridors. Bobby stood atop a chair and nervously unwound the screws holding the damaged vent in place. Passing the screws down to Kurt, he very gingerly pulled it away for a better look inside. Kurt passed him up a small torch and he swung the beam this way and that through the dark tunnel.

"Anything?" asked Kurt.

"Not even a web. These guys have to be long gone from here, right?"

"I assume so purely on the grounds that would make it a pain in the ass for all of us – and I know never to expect anything to be easy."

"Hey, don't be so negative. A scientific discovery pretty much fell into our laps."

"Right. And then it fucked off again."

***

Anna and Jazmin had the office block, consisting of the Captain's office, several archive rooms, and a large stationery cupboard. Anna was laying on the floor with a torch, trying to get a look under desks and furniture, hopeful for even a glimpse of something that might indicate the spiders had been this way.

"Goddamn it, I knew this would be hard, but this is a needle in a haystack."

Jazmin was going slow, easing lids off of archive boxes as if she expected one of the tarantulas to leap up and onto her face in a flash of legs and teeth. "You really think they could be up here?"

"It's one of the more consistently warm areas, plus it's up near the top where heat rises. On a good day I can work in here in a t-shirt, rather than wrapped up in coats and blankets. So, going on what we know both about invertebrates and creatures from days of yore, they're going to seek out the heat."

Jazmin hefted the archive box she'd been working on top of a shelf, and grabbed another. "So, where are the most likely places for them to hide? On Tempest Outpost, I mean."

"Here, of course. Cameron and Roger are searching around the control room."

"The control room for the Prospero?"

"Yeah. It's exposed, so it can get cold, but Cameron spends so much time there that the heat is nearly always on. Sometimes you go in there and it's like a sauna, so I figured they could be attracted there. Claire and Betty are down in the boiler rooms. If they'll be anywhere, they'll be there. So Claire can find them."

"You don't like her much, do you?" asked Jazmin, raising an eyebrow.

"I like her fine."

"So, why did you send her to the place they're most likely to be, when you know she was downright terrified of them?"

"I don't like people griping when there's a job to do."

"I'm not griping, I'm just trying to underst-"

"Not you. Claire. No-one *likes* tarantulas, Jazmin; certainly no-one normal. And we all knew we were going to have to pitch in, yet she was the only one who threw a hissy fit about it. So, if one of them lands on her, and gives her a scare, or she ends up with a mouthful of web and gets grossed out, then that's a fair punishment as far as I'm concerned."

Jazmin pried open the lid of the archive box and let out a scream, falling backwards and upending the whole thing. Anna rushed over, helping her up and away.

"What is it? Did you see one?"

"It's there!" yelled Jazmin, stabbing at the pile of papers with her finger.

Anna looked down and saw the upside down spider. With its legs pulled in, it was roughly the size of a baked potato. "Is it dead?"

"I don't know! I remember something about how some spiders play dead by lying upside down!"

Anna pulled a pen from her pocket and jabbed the spider. A leg fell off and a dribble of black dust fell from the socket. "It's dead. Desiccated."

"Box it up. We can take it straight to the lab."

"We'll box it up, but we'll keep looking. If there's one, there could be more in here."

"Fuck, I hope not."

***

The massive latch to the boiler room clanked, and Betty put her shoulder to it to ease it open. It took two or three good, hard shoves before it let out a squeal and she staggered through into the dark boiler room. Claire followed behind her nervously.

"Jesus, this is horrible."

Betty pulled her hood down and ran a hand through her cropped hair, scanning the walls with a torch, looking for a light switch. "It's just neglected. No one ever comes down here. Think about your boiler at home; you probably only check in on that once in a blue moon, or when you think there might be a problem with it."

"Yeah, I guess. Man, it's hot in here."

"Well, yeah, this is where we get our hot water, what were you expecting?"

Claire scanned the darkness with her torch. The damp floor passed between several huge heating tanks, and the beam of light faded long before it hit the other wall.

"How large is this place?"

"It's pretty big."

"And we're hoping to find spiders here?"

"Spiders that might not even be here in the first place, yeah. But hey, it beats real work, we've got each other, and I've got a couple of joints in my pocket."

Claire laughed. "You sound like you're skiving off on a school trip, you know that?"

Betty found the light switch and hit it. The strip lights flickered for a moment, causing Claire to think she was seeing flickers of movement in the shadows, until they finally came on with a sullen yellow glow.

"Bulbs are old. Like I said – nobody really comes down here."

Claire shivered and looked up and around. "Should we stick together?"

The horror movie fan in Betty was unable to resist the temptation. "No, let's split up. We can do more damage that way."

"I knew you were going to say something like that. Okay, I'll check this central aisle. Where are you going?"

Betty shrugged before gesturing off down to her left. "This way I guess. We've not got walkie-talkies, so you'll have to scream if you find one."

"No worries there."

Claire undid her coat in the hot air of the boiler room and trod carefully down the corridor. Her brain was filled constantly with visions of finding the spiders on the floor, tucked under corridors, or dropping into her hair. She physically shivered at the idea that one could be on the back of her coat right now and she'd never know.

Betty had only taken a few steps down the left hand corridor when she came to a sudden halt and whispered, "Holy shit…"

Stretched all around her, spinning up to the rafters and back into the darkness, was a colossal web of whitish grey threads. In places, the webs were so thick that it was like a cheesy ghost train ride she remembered from childhood. Dust and iron oxide flakes had already gathered in patches, and a couple of small pouch like lumps indicated where some of Tempest Outpost's mice had come to a grisly end.

"This is unreal…" she whispered, scanning around with her torch.

The tarantula squatting in the web above her stretched its forelegs as the beam of light reflected in its eyes. It knew that this creature was far too large to serve as food, but it also knew that there was some other purpose it could serve. Crawling forward, it spat a web from its spinnerets and lowered itself directly above her. The occasional warm air current was not strong enough to throw it off course and it landed softly on Betty's shoulder.

The padding on her winter coat was too thick for the engineer to notice the tarantula as it crept slowly forward, and she was only able to offer up a slight gasp as its teeth sank into her neck and pumped in a shot of venom.

Betty dropped to her knees and slapped a hand to the wound. The tarantula rolled from her neatly onto the floor and hurriedly scurried up the wall and back into the web.

Ice cold pain lanced from the spider bite for a moment, and it took Betty a second or two to get her breath back. Standing, she gathered her torch from the floor where she had dropped it, and went in search of Claire.

Claire had made it past a couple of the boiler tanks, still treading very carefully, when Betty caught up with her. "Oh, hey. You find anything?"

"Nah," said Betty. "There's nothing here. No sign of them."

"You're sure? We haven't checked very far."

Betty shrugged it off. "Look, neither of us want to be here. Let's just pretend we searched. Like Cameron said, they'll all be dead in a day or two anyway."

"You're sure?"

Betty smiled. "Of course, I'm sure. Look let's just have a smoke and say we worked hard."

"You're a bad influence on me, Betty Harper."

"I'm a bad influence on everybody."

TEN

Betty took Claire back to her rooms, and lit up the joint from her pocket. "You really pulled the shittiest, shortest straw on this run, huh?"

"It's not so bad."

"Come on, I know girls like you. You like to work in a shiny glass office wearing nice skirt suits and sexy heels. You don't get into a job like yours so you can crawl around the boiler room of an oil rig in the South Pole. What'd you do? Royally piss off someone in the office?"

Claire laughed and took the offered joint. "No, actually I volunteered. I hadn't seen Anna in a long time and, well, I thought the idea of six weeks away from the office sounded like fun. Plus, how many people get a chance to go to the South Pole?"

Betty put some music on the stereo – some ambient, progressive thing – and threw herself down into a bean bag on the floor. "Yeah, I guess that's true. Your boyfriend not mind that he's got a month and half with no…you know?"

"Ha! I'm sure he'll find some way of entertaining himself. Anna asked the same thing, and I said football, Xbox and beer."

"That's pretty much how we cope out here. Well, porn, weed and PlayStation for me, but the overall vibe is the same."

Betty's eyes flickered to the tarantula climbing up the wall behind Claire, and said nothing. Claire took another deep drag and passed the joint back to her, slumping back against the wall. "I am so tired, Betty. The jet lag and the flight and the spiders and...ugh. I just want to sleep for days."

The tarantula slowly began crawling along toward her. Betty shrugged. "Well, why don't you have a sleep here? We've got a couple of hours – at least – before we need to go back and report on everything we found."

"You sure you don't mind?"

"Sure. I promise I won't feel you up or anything."

Claire giggled, closing her eyes. "That's a shame."

The music and the weed and the warmth conspired together to make a virtual blanket, and she lay her head back against the wall, her brain already fogging with the aching comfort on the borders of sleep. She tried to concentrate on the music, and it gradually grew muffled as her brain slowly began to shut down and rest.

She was mostly asleep when she felt Betty's fingers on her shoulder. Maybe she had thought Claire had been joking when she said it was a shame she wasn't going to feel her up. She gently tilted her head to one side to expose more of her neck, and she felt the small fingertips crawl softly across her skin. The corner of her mouth involuntarily tugged in a smile and the hairs on her arm rose. She was just about to say something – though she had no idea what – when a terrible pain shot through her neck, spasming up into her lower jaw and ear, and down to her shoulder. The pain felt ice cold, as though she had trapped a nerve while buried in snow. She let out a strangled cry and came fully awake in time to see the spider that had bitten her run up the wall and squat in the corner of the ceiling.

She slapped her hand to her neck and saw that her palm came away bloody. "Fuck! Betty, what the fuck!"

She looked over at Betty and felt a panic attack coming on. Betty was sitting there, impassive, as if waiting for something to happen. What? Had Betty known the spider was there all the time? Had she even…?

Claire relaxed back into the beanbag and closed her eyes. The music and the weed and the warmth conspired together to make a virtual blanket, and she lay her head back against the wall, her brain already fogging with the aching comfort on the borders of sleep. She tried to concentrate on the music, and it gradually grew muffled as her brain slowly began to shut down and rest.

The tarantula waited for a moment, then crawled down the wall, and back into Betty's hoodie pocket, savouring the warmth.

***

The crew of Tempest Outpost gathered around one of the tables in the canteen, which seemed to have been adopted as a meeting room. Captain Anna rubbed her eyes wearily and groaned raspily in her throat. "So, Jazmin and I managed to find one of these chitinous bastards dead in an archive box."

Jazmin placed a Tupperware containing the desiccated spider on the table. Those who hadn't yet seen the spiders leaned forward eagerly.

"It's weird," said Roger. "Tarantulas are normally hairy. This dude is totally hairless. It makes him look less like a tarantula and just like a...like a giant spider."

Kurt nodded. "Agreed. If it's okay with you, Captain, I'd like to take this dead one for dissection."

"Fine by me. Just make sure it's dead – and even if it is, make sure it can't come back to life," said Anna, dismissively.

"Yes, ma'am."

"So, no-one saw anything? No-one saw so much as a web?"

Everyone around the table muttered a negative or shook their heads.

"I'm open to suggestions."

Cameron raised his hand, and Anna nodded for him to go ahead. "I'd like to fire up the Prospero again, Captain. We've found one of these things dead already, which reinforces my faith in my original proposition that these things will have a very short life span. The other three are either dead or dying, likely due to the difference in climate between the Pre-Hadean era of the planet and a drilling rig in the South Pole."

"Right? Who knew?"

"However, we don't know what's happening at the bottom of the ocean below us. For all we know there could be more of these

– or other similar creatures – that are dying, dissolving, decomposing…"

Betty spoke up. "That sounds like a very good idea to me. We should definitely bring up some more samples."

Claire nodded along. "Yeah. I mean, if these things aren't dead and have set up a nest somewhere, then we should have some we can study and learn from. We need more of them up here."

Captain Anna raised an eyebrow. "You've changed your tune. You've hated having these things on board since they arrived."

Claire shrugged. "I want to be forewarned. If we have more onboard, Cam, Kurt, Roger and Jazmin can analyse the things. We can at least work out if they're venomous or not. I mean…if they're not venomous I'll sleep easier, won't you?"

Betty nodded. "And they could all just…be dying down there, like Cameron said. If we have discovered a new species, don't we have a duty of care to it? We can't just smash up where they were hibernating and then leave them to a cold, black death."

Anna rubbed her eyes tiredly. "I don't really give a fuck about them, to be honest."

"Icecap Industries, will," said Claire.

"Excuse me?"

"We've found a wholly new species here. If you don't think Icecap Industries will attach a significant dollar value to that discovery, then you're just plain being naive. And I'm the one who's here to investigate how this rig is being run."

Anna stared daggers at Claire. "I see. So, what you're saying is that if I don't authorise another drilling, you're going to report back to Icecap that I fucked Tempest's reason to be here?"

"I'm saying I'll be doing my job. You should be doing yours."

The atmosphere in the room had gone decidedly cold. After a couple of seconds, Jazmin broke the silence. "Look, we're all really tired and stressed over this whole deal. Sure, I can understand what Claire's saying but…Claire, what if Anna authorises the drilling and it turns out that these things are venomous and alive and running around, possibly breeding. The Captain would be in even more trouble with Icecap for letting one of their rigs become basically one big spider's web. I'm with her – on the side of caution – here."

Anna maintained her glare on Claire. "I'll sleep on it, and make a decision in the morning. The 'fossils' didn't hatch until they warmed up, so I don't think they're in any danger down there, do you? It's late, we're all tired, and we can tackle this in the morning. Everyone's dismissed. If anyone wants to help me blow off some stress, I'll be at the *Street Fighter II* machine with a box of Twinkies."

Cameron stood up. "I'm game."

The rest of the crew squeaked their chairs back from the table, and headed off in separate directions. The spider in Betty's pocket huddled its legs under its belly, and bided its time.

ELEVEN

Kurt didn't head back to his rooms. He went to the lab to continue typing up some notes on the fossils and spiders they had found. The strip lighting flickered into life and he booted up the computer, dropping wearily into the seat. The coffee he'd left on the desk before the meeting was cold, but he couldn't find the energy to make another cup, instead grabbing a can of Pepsi Max from the drawer of his desk. He managed to just miss the tarantula clinging to the underside of his desk as it scurried closer.

His report was a little scattered, and – in places – rather ambiguous. Truth be told, the discovery of the spiders had rattled him rather a lot. He understood the significance of their discovery, and in a philosophical sense, it felt very much as though the rug had been pulled from under him. Every single thing he had learned about geology and the evolution of the entire planet could be thrown into disarray if this was shown to be correct.

The meeting itself had rattled him, too. He didn't want to be in a position where he would be forced to take a side in the debate. He could see the benefits of firing the Prospero a second time, but he also understood the need for caution. Of course, if a second drilling did bring up more geode like objects, they'd all be better prepared to deal with them. Lock and seal them in vivaria straight away. Were there vivaria on board? Possibly. If not they'd improvise and demand that Icecap send some straight away, and screw the expense.

The species we have discovered I have named Theraphosidae Caliban, although aboard Tempest Outpost, they have already earned the common names "Ice Spiders" and "The Tarantulas". They certainly appear to be tarantulas, although due to their condition (ie. Fossilised) at the time of discovery, it was not possible to conduct a full examination to confirm this.

One key difference was noticeable, however, which was the absence of any hairs of the type normally associated with your typical tarantula. Many tarantulas are capable of firing urticating hairs from their abdomen as a defensive weapon. The absence of such hairs on the Ice Spiders have three possible explanations – firstly, that the hair is typically present, but was lost during the hibernation/fossilisation process. Secondly, that these are not true tarantulas, but rather large spiders, or something else entirely. Thirdly, and possibly most terrifyingly, that these creatures have no predators in their natural habitat, and as such have no need for any kind of defensive weapon.

Kurt let out a strangled cry as a white lance of pain shot from his knee cap up his thigh and radiated down his calf. His leg spasmed involuntarily, and he kicked out backwards, falling off his chair. His eyes fell instantly to the tarantula squatting under the desk, and he knew instantly that he had been bitten by the monstrous thing. He scrambled to his feet, desperate to find something to capture or kill the beast with.

Snatching up a plastic beaker, he turned back to the computer and tried to remember what it was that he had been doing. He had needed the beaker for something, but it eluded him now. He set the beaker next to his cold coffee, and righted his chair. Sitting back at the computer, he deleted the last five pages of his write up on the Ice Spiders, saved it, and rubbed his eyes wearily.

***

Roger could barely hear the sound of banging on his door over the sound of the Afrika Bambaataa he was blasting through his 100w speaker set up. Blasting some classic hip-hop vinyl was his favourite way of relaxing. He was far too young to have been around for Afrika the first time, of course, but his father had raised him on Afrika Bambaataa, Grandmaster Flash and Kurtis Flow. He found it comforting to throw up a wall of noise like this. It isolated him from the stress and strains of the day job, but it also made him feel as though he was closer to his home and family, rather than marooned in a rattly rig off the coast of Antarctica. Eventually, during a break beat, he heard the banging on the door, and dropped the volume down before answering it. He was expecting Betty – the two of them often hung out after hours, smoking weed and watching movies – or the Captain, who liked his music.

Claire stood at his door. She'd changed into a pair of tight jeans and a white hoodie, and in her hand was a six pack of Red Stripe lager, the metal prickling with condensation. "I'm bored, I found this in the stores, and I heard *Planet Rock*. Cool if I hang out?"

Roger raised his eyebrow, but quickly smiled. "Yeah, of course you can. Everyone is welcome here; especially if they dig Afrika and bring beers."

Claire danced past him as he stepped back to allow her in. The Captain allowed all of the crew to spread out across several rooms so that they lived in mini-apartments, rather than the single bed allotted to a standard oil rig crew, but this didn't change the fact that some of the original build structure was rather cramped. Claire popped open a can of lager and passed another to Roger. He accepted it gratefully and laughed.

"You didn't strike me as a hip-hop fan when I first saw you."

"Oh? And what do you see me being into?"

"I dunno, man. Not this stuff, though."

Claire threw herself down onto his couch and took a long drink of the Red Stripe. "I got in via Public Enemy and Run DMC and worked backwards."

Roger sat next to her. "Ah, those guys are great. My Dad got me into Afrika. It was just always on, you know. I'll have to tell him I met a fellow fan in the Antarctic."

Claire laughed, and they chatted about music as the tarantula crawled out of her hoodie pocket, and across the floor toward Roger's ankle.

***

Jazmin had been flicking through the options on the oil rig's movie package when she heard the knock on her door. She was a little confused at first, then realised any of the crew could be stopping by to ask her to jump back on the clock. It could be something in the laboratory, or perhaps the spiders had resurfaced. She swung her legs down from her top bunk, dropping to the floor with a thud, and opened the door.

Betty, the short haired engineer stood there, leaning against the door frame. "Hey."

"Uh...hey," said Jazmin. "What's up?"

Betty shrugged, and Jazmin saw she was holding a six pack of Red Stripe lager in one hand. "I was just bored, figured you might be stuck for something to do, as you're finding your feet here...wondered if you wanted to hang out and do a movie? You like horror movies?"

"I...uh...sometimes. Sure. I'd love to hang out, but maybe another night. I'm really tired, this spider thing got me on edge, and I'm just looking to crash out, to be honest."

Betty leaned in a little, and Jazmin wondered if this was more of a come-on than a social call. "Ah, come on. Just one movie, a couple of beers...I got a couple of bifters in my pocket, too."

"I dunno, Betty. Like I say, I'm really tired. Give me a couple of days, maybe."

"You sure?"

"Yeah, I'm sorry. I appreciate the offer, I really do, but I'm just beyond tired."

Betty shrugged. "No worries. I'll see if anyone else is up and fancies it."

Jazmin felt bad for rejecting the woman, and tried to kick some life back into the conversation. "So, what movies do you recommend?"

"You like horror movies?"

"Sure. Sometimes. I get scared if I watch them alone, though."

"Best you save those for when you've got someone to cuddle up to then," joked Betty with a wink, making Jazmin blush. "Ah, I'm just messing with you."

"No, it's cool. I'd like a movie night with you sometime."

Betty nodded. "Sounds cool. Here."

She reached back and handed Betty a joint from behind her ear. "This'll help you sleep if nothing else. Don't watch any scary movies without me, though. It sucks if paranoia kicks in. When I was sixteen I got way too fucking high and watched *Poltergeist* all on my own. That was a bad idea. When I had to go the toilet before bed, I kept my eyes to the floor so I didn't have to see my own reflection in the bathroom mirror."

"Why's that?"

"You've never seen *Poltergeist*?"

"No, never."

"We'll make it the opening feature for our movie night, then. Anyway, it's been good to talk to you. See you tomorrow."

"See you."

Jazmin locked her bedroom door and took the joint over to the window. Perhaps this and a gentle romantic comedy was what she needed.

The spider in Betty's jacket pocket let out a hiss of dissatisfaction, and curled into a ball to sleep.

TWELVE

After the breakfast meeting, Captain Anna sat with her head in her hands. She had expected the vote to be a total landslide. Surely none of them could want more spiders running around. She thought that Cameron – for sure – would want to use the Prospero again, but that thing was his baby. He'd fire it up and play with it every day if he could. Both Betty and Roger had been in favour of another drilling, and they were the opposite of Cameron in terms of motivation. Another drilling meant more work for them, and they would normally do anything for an easy life.

Kurt hadn't been so much of a surprise. He wanted more samples to play with. And Claire obviously hadn't changed her mind from the previous day. So that had left just her, Jazmin and Bobby voting against another drilling. So, the next morning, the Prospero would once again go spinning down into the ocean to bring up god knows what sea monsters lay below.

She felt a hand on her shoulder and looked up to see Jazmin. "You okay?"

"No, not really. I'm sure it'll be fine, though. I just…I didn't expect this when I accepted the job, you know? Fossils, sure. Rocks that look normal to us but are somehow endlessly fascinating to Kurt and Bobby and Cameron – and, I guess, you – absolutely. Hell, maybe even oil, should we be so lucky. I didn't expect monstrous undead spiders."

Jazmin slid into a seat next to her. "We're out on the frontier here. We shouldn't know what to expect."

"Yeah, I know. I just…I guess I expected the discoveries to be boring. And actually they're terrifying. And now things are getting weirder. I honestly didn't think Betty and Roger would want to go drilling. For them, the longer that goes between drillings then the happier they are. They only really have work to do every time we fire it up. Don't get me wrong, when there's work that needs doing, they do it and they do it well and they do a thorough job; but all the same, they'd rather there was no work to do and they could sit on their backsides listening to music and watching movies."

"Does Betty seem to be acting unusual to you?"

"How do you mean?"

Jazmin nervously played with her fingers. "She, uh, came by my room last night. I mean, don't get me wrong, it was friendly, and kind of flattering, but it was just…I don't think she'd said more than twenty words to me before now."

"I see. What did she want?"

"I dunno. She made it sound like we could just hang out and watch movies, but there was definitely an undertone of something else there, if you follow me."

Anna shrugged and took a sip of coffee. "Maybe she likes you."

"Claire seems strange, too."

"That she does."

"The other day she was practically climbing the walls because she was so scared of the tarantulas running around. Now, she's the one pushing the lead to light up the Prospero and potentially bring up a whole damned horde of the things."

Anna rubbed her eyes wearily. "That I had noticed, too."

"You think something strange is going on, don't you?"

"Yeah. Yeah, I do. Do you think that the Prospero could have brought up more than just the spiders?"

"How do you mean?"

Anna kicked back from her chair and started pacing the length of the table. "I don't know. It's just...everyone acting out of character so suddenly. Could some weird gas have been released when the geodes cracked, or something? I mean, carbon monoxide or something. Well, not carbon monoxide, but you know what I'm getting at right?"

Jazmin shook her head. "I'm with you that something downright weird is happening here, but I'm not sure it's down to something like that. We need to talk to people, find out what's going on."

"You're right. I'll try and get a hold of Betty, see if we can have a word with her in my office. She'll probably think I'm going to give her a scolding for trying to chat you up last night, so we may be able to catch her off guard."

"Okay."

***

Betty shuffled into Anna's office, lit cigarette in hand. "You wanted to see me, Captain?"

Anna sat at her desk, playing with a pen. Jazmin stood just behind her, looking nervous. "I absolutely do, Miss Harper. Don't panic, though. I'm going to see everyone today; I just want to do so individually, so as no-one influences each other."

"Huh. Okay. What's on your mind, Captain?"

"What's your reasoning behind wanting to use the Prospero again?"

Betty looked confused for a moment before replying. "We need to bring up more of the geodes."

Jazmin and Anna flashed a glance at each other.

"And why is that so important?" asked Anna.

"It's why we're here isn't it?"

"We're here to test the Prospero and to examine any rocks or other material it unearths. Why do you think the geodes specifically are so important?"

"Because of the spiders."

"You think this is a case of animal welfare?"

Betty shook her head and her eyes glazed oddly. "I don't know. Look, I just...feel...we need to bring up more stuff. What if the spiders we found are just the proverbial tip of the iceberg? We need to know what's down there, Captain."

Captain Anna walked around her desk and stood directly in front of the engineer. "What's going on Betty?"

"Nothing."

"What's going on, Betty?"

"I told you: nothing. We're here to do a job, and that's what we should be doing. We need to bring up more of the spiders."

"Bullshit. You're bone idle, Harper. You don't do shit unless you have to, and now you want to give yourself a shit ton of work so you can bring up a load of rocks you're not interested in? I don't buy it for a goddamned second. You don't want to fire up the drill. You want to smoke weed and watch horror movies in your room until your shift is up."

"I'm on a long shift. Nothing for me at home."

"Whatever. My point remains. So, once again, who is 'she' and why do we need her so badly?"

Betty's eyes glazed over, she balled her fists and thrust her face into Anna's. "Go fuck yourself, Captain."

Anna struck Betty across the face with a crack, and Jazmin gasped. "Stow that shit, Betty. Get yourself to your quarters. I'm calling an evac for you immediately. You're obviously ill."

Betty let out a strangled noise and reached into her pocket. When she withdrew her hand, Anna screamed and fell backwards. The vile, white tarantula on the engineer's palm threw up its front legs and flexed its teeth in a show of aggression. It tensed its back legs and leapt onto Anna, crawling rapidly up her chest.

Acting quickly, Jazmin ran to Betty, span her around, and socked her hard across the jaw. Betty's head snapped back then forward almost straight away, and Jazmin saw stars as the engineer connected with a headbutt across the bridge of her nose. Staggered, Jazmin grabbed Betty and threw her hard to the floor. She skidded and screamed as the bare flesh of her neck came into contact with the office's electric radiator. She slapped a hand to the burnt area and looked around confused. "What? What the fuck?"

Anna screamed as the tarantula scurried up her chest and towards her neck. Grabbing hold of some papers that had fallen from her desk in the scuffle, she batted it away. It fell onto its back and skidded along the floor. Quickly righting itself, it ran across the floor back towards Betty. Betty let out a scream at the thing's approach and kicked her legs out at it. In her panic she missed again and again, until suddenly – with a squeal and a crunch – Jazmin's boot struck down and pulverised it.

Anna gasped for breath and pulled herself into a sitting position against the desk. Betty held her hand against the burn on her neck and groaned. "Where the fuck did that thing come from?"

Jazmin lifted up her boot, showing smashed chitin and a strange grey, black powder. She had been expecting goo and gore, but it was as though the thing had turned to a fossil again –

it was just smashed rock on the inside. "You're kidding right? What the fuck were you doing bringing that thing in here?"

"What? What do you mean? I didn't! We were talking and then…did one of you hit me?"

THIRTEEN

Betty clambered to her feet, still rubbing the burned spot on her neck, Jazmin wiped her boot clean on the carpet, and Anna staggered to her chair as the three women tried to make sense of what had happened.

"Do you remember coming to my room last night?" asked Jazmin.

"Kinda. I mean, yeah, but...until you mentioned it, not really. It's like you reminded me of a dream I had."

"Did you see the spider go into your pocket?"

"What? No. Eww." Betty shakily lit a cigarette. "I'm just glad that's two down, two to go."

"They must have some sort of mesmeric influence," said Jazmin. "I mean, you don't remember coming in here, you don't remember visiting me last night, you don't remember throwing the tarantula at the Captain?"

"I did? Uh...sorry about that."

Captain Anna waved the apology away. "If this is true, then anyone else who voted in favour of using the drill again could be under the influence of the spiders. The spiders must want more of them up here, and the best way of doing that is to use the Prospero. That's why so many people wanted to use it. Shit...so that means..."

"Who voted in favour of using it?" asked Betty.

Jazmin helped herself to one of Betty's cigarettes. "You, Kurt, Roger, Claire and Cameron."

"So all of them are under the influence of the spiders?"

Anna shook her head. "We don't know that. They might just want to use the drill again for reasons of their own. Betty, what happened to make you come back to your senses? When we killed the spider?"

"No. I remember seeing Jazmin step on it. I don't think that made much of a difference. It was..."

She rubbed at the sore, burned spot on the back of her neck. "When I hit the radiator. It was like a slap to the face, or being dunked in ice cold water. It just snapped me out of it. I remember clearly coming to the office because you called me...then everything is like a half remembered dream...then I burnt myself on the radiator."

Anna rubbed her eyes tiredly. "I don't want to go around the rig burning everyone who voted against my decision. That will look very bad on a CV."

"We'll try Kurt first. He's a big guy, and once we've tried him, well...he might be helpful in snapping back the others," said Jazmin.

Betty rubbed her face. "Seriously, did one of you hit me?"

***

Anna, Jazmin and Betty marched into the laboratory where Kurt and Bobby were working. The two geologists were surprised to see them all together.

"Oh. Hello, ladies," said Bobby, looking up from a microscope. "What can we help you with?"

"We need a word with Kurt.," said Betty, lighting a cigarette.

"Uh, okay…you probably shouldn't smoke in here, though."

Kurt looked up from his desk and Anna and Jazmin straight away noticed the oddly glazed look in his eyes that Betty had had before attacking them with the tarantula. They heard Betty's breath catch as she realised how she must have looked to them both. Anna crossed her arms and stood in front of Kurt.

"Why do you want to try drilling the area again?"

"We need to bring up more samples. Those other spiders are long gone by now. I'm sure there's no danger."

"I didn't mention anything about there being any danger. How about I say okay but we hold off on it for a day or two? Really make sure these other spiders are good and dead."

Kurt bolted to his feet. "No! You can't do that! They need more of their kind. We need to rescue them *now!*"

Anna gave a nod to Betty and she stabbed down on Kurt's hand with the lit end of her cigarette. Kurt yelped in shock and pain, grabbing his hand. "What the fuck did you do that for?"

"Kurt, how would you feel about holding off on another drilling for a few days?"

"Jesus, Betty…what the fuck? What? Why would I care about that? We've still got loads to do here. Those geodes have waited for a few billion years! What's another couple of days?"

Anna clapped him on the arm. "It's good to have you back, Kurt."

***

"Jesus fucking Christ what the fucking fuck did you do that for?" demanded Cameron, clutching at the cigarette burn on the back of his hand.

"Tell us why you want to use the Prospero again."

"Because it's my life's work? Jesus fuck, Captain…"

"You still want to use it?" asked Jazmin.

"Yeah, of course. I want to see what else is down there! Am I the only one who realises that we made a scientific and historical fucking breakthrough yesterday? And now you're kicking in my door and burning me with cigarettes? What the hell is going on?"

The captain clapped him on the shoulder in a show of affection. "Just a hunch that didn't pay off. Long story short, we thought that you were under the mental control of some spiders from Earth's distant past, but it turns out you're just kind of an asocial dick. Which is good news all round. See you for dinner."

The three women left him alone, the door shutting with a percussive click.

"You know I could have told you that without you having to torture me!"

***

"You can't find them? What the hell do you mean you can't find them? We got to look harder!"

Bobby reached up and gently pulled Captain Anna down into her chair again. He, Kurt and Cameron had gone looking for Roger and Claire, but they couldn't be found anywhere. "Ease down, Captain. They could be anywhere, doing anything. She's not in her place, but…well…Roger's door was locked. They could just be…well…you know."

"She's not his type," said Betty, lighting a cigarette.

"How do you mean?"

"He doesn't go for white girls."

"I guess that means you weren't his type either," joked Kurt.

"*He* was never mine."

They all jumped as Anna thumped her fist down on the table. "Look, something weird is going on on this rig and it *all* comes back to those geodes and those spiders. I want the last two found, and now it turns out that two members of my crew have gone missing, too. That concerns me. As one of them wasn't technically a member of my crew, is totally new to the area, and represents a large part of our funding, it concerns me greatly. I want those last two spiders, I want Roger and I want Claire. If you've got to break down Roger's door, I'll gladly pay for the repairs out of my own pocket. I don't care. I just want them *found*."

Betty stubbed out a cigarette and reached for her coffee. "Okay, let's assume the worst case scenario – which is that they are under the influence of the Spiders from Mars, here. You ever gone for a wander down in the depths? I mean like the real 'engine room' stuff we've got here? If someone wants to stay hidden, then down in the gears and machines…you'd be undetectable."

"Are the spiders capable of projecting that much mental influence?" asked Cameron, who'd wrapped up his hand in rather an excessive bandage.

"We don't know," said Jazmin. "We're dealing with the total unknown."

Kurt spoke up. "Speaking for myself – and I assume Betty felt the same – I had no idea I was under any influence at all. Even now it seems like a half remembered dream."

He looked across to Betty who nodded her assent.

"I'd guess there are limits," said Cameron. "I mean, you say that your notes are gone from the computer? Okay, assume the spiders made you do that – why didn't they go the whole hog and make you smash up the entire lab? Surely that would have been a more thorough job."

"That's easy," replied Bobby. "Camouflage."

"How do you mean?"

"Kurt smashing up the lab would have set alarm bells ringing. Him just deleting files from the computer? It could have been weeks or months before we found that. The spiders don't want to do anything that draws attention to themselves."

Cameron nodded. "That makes a sort of sense. Something like a trapdoor spider of the mind."

Anna tore open a Twinkie box. "A lovely turn of phrase. Back to the case – what to do next?"

"I think I know where the spiders are," said Jazmin.

"You do?"

"They have to be where Betty and Claire originally searched. That's how the spiders got her and Claire. Roger was with Cameron, and Cameron wasn't affected. Kurt was with Bobby and Bobby wasn't affected. Therefore it's the only option that makes sense."

"The boiler room," said Betty.

FOURTEEN

Anna nominated Bobby and Cameron to check out the boiler room. She didn't think it fair to throw Jazmin into a potentially dangerous situation, and she knew for sure that neither Cameron nor Bobby had ever been under the influence of the spiders. Betty was brave, and Kurt was large, but she didn't wholly trust them to deal with either the spiders or potentially dangerous members of her crew. Who knew what remnants of the spiders' power could still hang over them?

Bobby carried a large torch to penetrate the gloom, and Cameron carried a crowbar he'd found, in case things did turn nasty. Bobby put his shoulder to the door and forced it open with a protesting squeal.

"Was that you, or the door?" joked Cameron.

Bobby dropped his voice to a whisper. "Shut up, man. If the two zombies, or the spiders are in here, then the last thing I want to do is warn them we're coming."

"Because they won't have heard the door anyway?"

"Shut up, Cam."

Bobby swept his torch across the corridor that greeted them. "Do we want to split up?"

"Are you serious? In what horror movie is that ever a good idea?"

"Good thinking."

The darkness around them was all encompassing. The sun shone weakly through the door they had entered through, but it seemed afraid of the blackness inside. Bobby stepped inside and swung his torch left, right and up and down. "Man, this place is big. It looks like it shouldn't able to fit on the rig, never mind in this little corner."

"That's quality engineering for you, man," said Cameron, following him through. "So, do we go left, right or straight ahead?"

"Let's go left, then work our way across."

"All right."

Their footsteps seemed amplified in the large, echoing chamber of the boiler room. Every touch of their boots on the gantry floor seemed to shudder across its entire length, and it triggered a million silken tripwires, alerting the remaining spiders to the intruders' arrival. Cameron kept the beam of the torch to the floor so that they didn't tread on, or trip over, anything.

"Why aren't there any lights in here?" he whispered.

"There probably are – it's just I can't remember how to switch them on."

Bobby came to an abrupt stop as he saw the webbing stretched across the floor in front of him. "What the fuck is this?"

The webbing wasn't just like the thin strands of a spider web you find in any corner of a house, or even the thick cushioned bedding he'd seen tarantulas make in zoos and pet shops. It was so thick it was almost like woven material; as thick as a carpet or curtain. He swept the torch up and down, and saw that the webbing continued up the walls and onto the high ceiling. He slowly brought the beam back to the floor and looked to see how far it continued. The entire floor was carpeted for the length of the corridor.

"My god. They moved in," whispered Cameron. "In less than twenty-four hours they colonised the boiler room. Of course! It's warm here. They can…oh fuck…"

"What?"

Cameron grabbed Bobby's arm and swung the beam of the torch to a point just ahead of them, about seven feet up from the floor. "How could they have done all this so quickly?"

"It's a totally new species, Cam. We don't have a damn clue."

Bobby lowered the beam further and let out a full scream.

The torchlight had come to rest on the face of Claire Flynn, wrapped up tight in the webbing. Her skin was pale and her eyes closed. The webbing stretched across her neck, through her hair, and partially across her mouth.

Cameron slapped Bobby and whispered, "Keep your fucking voice down."

"Fuck you, man!" Bobby whispered back. "Is she dead?"

Cameron reached forward, and touched her neck, feeling for a pulse. "Yeah. She's cold."

"We've got to get the fuck out of here, man. Let's go get everyone else, and come back here in a group to burn this whole fucking thing down."

Cameron backed away slowly. "Yeah. That sounds like a real fucking good idea."

Bobby turned away from the dead woman and let out another scream as he walked straight into Roger. "Jesus fucking Christ, Roger. You scared the hell out of me. How long have you been dow-?"

Bobby didn't get to finish his sentence as Roger's utility knife flashed up and into his neck. Bobby let out a coughing gargle, and dropped to his knees, clutching at his throat to stem the flow of blood. The torch bounced and rolled across the floor, and Cameron saw the nest in white light pulses of nightmare. He saw Roger pull Bobby up by his hair and stab him twice more. He saw the geodes swinging in their web. He saw the ghostly face of Claire flash by, and he saw three of the spiders crawling down the wall towards him. He swung at them with the crowbar, ripping the wall of webbing and sending them flying.

He shoved hard at Roger. "Fuck's sake, man! What're you doing?"

Roger turned to him and his glazed over look told Cameron that he was fully under the control of the spiders now.

Hating himself for leaving, he went to turn and run from the boiler room when he suddenly felt arms around him. Claire had burst forth from the webbing wall and grabbed a hold of him. "Cameron...don't leave me..." she whispered. "Please..."

Cameron screamed again. "You...you're alive?"

"Please...get me out of here..."

Cameron became a hero for the first and last time in his life.

He spun around and cracked Roger across the back of the head with the crowbar. The large engineer flew into the thick webbing coating the walls and slumped over. Grabbing Claire around her waist, he ripped her legs free of the itchy, creepy silk and dragged her with him. She could barely walk so he had to haul her with him, her feet banging a rhythm of terror on the metal floor as he ran as fast as he could for the exit and its beacon of daylight.

Fearing that Roger or the spiders could follow him at any moment, he barreled through the doorway and helped Claire gently to the floor outside. He quickly pulled the door shut and slammed his shoulder into it. The door squeaked part of the way into place, but rust, disuse and salt spray had caused the door and frame to not fit quite so well as they should have. He slammed his shoulder into it again and again, squeezing it closer and closer each time; knowing that should Roger recover and force it from the other side, he wouldn't stand a chance.

A high pitched squeaking noise drew his attention and he saw one of the spiders in the open corner near the floor. Redoubling his efforts, he leapt up and threw his entire bodyweight into it and the door finally wedged shut, chitin and rock dust spraying from the crushed spider.

Cameron quickly threw the bar across the door and clicked the padlock home. Finally, with the immediate threat over, he fell to his backside and struggled to get his breath back.

"Cameron?" said Claire weakly. "Thank you."

Cameron struggled to his feet, every muscle aching, and helped Claire to stand. She leant into him, and he hugged her back. "It's okay, we're out of there now. Let's get back up to the Captain and the rest of the crew, and we can tell them all about what happened."

She pulled him closer to her. "I can't remember what happened. It's all like a dream. It's like I kind of half remembered it."

"Yeah, that's what the others said. Don't worry, you won't be alone. Kurt and Betty had similar run ins. You'll be okay."

"Where's the key to the padlock?"

"What? Why?"

"Where is it?"

Cameron was confused but didn't want to break the hug. "It's...uh...still in the lock. Don't worry, I'm sure none of the spiders can work a key."

"Okay."

Cameron saw her hair move gently to the side, assuming at first that it was the wind, but a microsecond later he saw the white legs and fangs of the spider that had ridden her shoulder the whole time. Its back legs tensed and it jumped forward. He pushed Claire away and fell hard on his backside, as the hideous thing crawled across his face. Its front legs and fangs hooked into his bottom lip and he felt it bite hard. Freezing pain ran down his jaw and neck as the ice spider pumped its venom in.

He looked to Claire for assistance and saw her unlocking the padlock. For a moment it felt to him as though that was a very bad idea. Then he got to his feet and helped her pull the door open, before following her back into the boiler room.

FIFTEEN

Jazmin and Betty pushed open the doors to the canteen, scaring the life out of Anna and Kurt, who had been waiting in nervous anticipation.

"We kicked down Roger's door," said Betty.

"Well, we took a fire axe to it."

"You're mouthy for a work experience kid, you know that? Anyway, yeah, we broke it down. No sign of Roger or Claire. Room looked, well…pretty normal to be honest. His room was usually organised chaos, you know, and there was nothing out of the ordinary there."

"So they're still missing?" said Kurt.

"I'm thinking 'missing presumed dead'," said Betty, lighting a cigarette. "Captain, we need back up here. We've got people missing. We've got weird, telepathic spiders. Now, this is the point where you're supposed to go Quint and smash up the radio. So I'm going to ask you very nicely not to do that, please."

"We should radio Icecap," agreed Captain Anna. "A few spiders in the air conditioning we could manage. This is getting beyond us."

"Hold on," said Kurt. "Shouldn't we wait for Cameron and Bobby to come back? They could have found them, or they may have news on the spiders themselves. I'm not against radioing for help, but I do think we should wait for all the information first."

Anna slumped into a chair. "You're right. We'll give them another twenty minutes. If they're not back by then, we radio Icecap for as much assistance as they can throw at us."

Jazmin shuffled uncomfortably over to another table and sat down. She didn't feel she could leave, but didn't want to sit down in the atmosphere around the Captain at the moment. It felt wrong to just be sat there waiting for news of the others, but there was nothing else to do. She sat, playing with her fingers nervously, and didn't know what to suggest. She looked up as Betty sat next to her and offered her a cigarette, which she accepted shakily.

"You don't smoke, do you?"

"I thought I might take it up."

"You want me to light it for you?"

"Uh...sure."

Betty lit the cigarette and passed it back to her. "Draw a small amount of smoke into your mouth – not too much, or you'll cough. Then take in some air and draw it all down into your lungs."

Jazmin did as she was taught. A couple of times she felt a cough twitch at her stomach like a hiccough, but she held it down.

"Then let it out."

Jazmin exhaled a cloud of smoke, and Betty smiled at her. She felt a little light headed, and a little more relaxed. Betty rested her hand on hers and said, "We're going to get out of here, you know. Don't worry."

***

Cameron unlocked the door to the control room, and swung it open vaingloriously. Claire followed him inside and watched as Cameron switched on the lights and began powering up the colossal control panel that occupied the span of the windows. She looked across the space in the centre of the rig, where the Prospero hung just above them.

"What do you need me to do?" asked Claire, rubbing absently at her hair, pulling out tufts of webbing.

"Nothing so far. You can just stand there and look pretty," said Cameron. His practiced hands danced across the control console, lighting up LEDs and causing gauges to flicker into life. "The thing's set up so that it can be operated from here. This is the brain, the nerve centre, of Prospero. The rest of Tempest Outpost is just a frame to hang it from."

"You think we'll bring up more eggs?"

"We both know we will."

"Yes."

The room buzzed and vibrated a little as Cameron pulled a lever that looked like a main circuit breaker. Claire lifted her eyes up and saw the Prospero begin to turn gently. "It's working."

"Of course it's working."

The massive drill bit began to twist faster and faster as Cameron threw switches, adjusted dials and jabbed at touchscreen interfaces.

"And…fire!"

Cameron hit the large red button, and the tone that had been resonating through the entire control room kicked into higher gear. The Prospero span and dropped down, past the window in front of them and down into the ocean. Claire flinched at the splash, which sprayed water droplets against the glass, even at this height. The barrel of the drill continued down into the ocean, and Cameron tracked its progress on the touchscreens.

"Five, four, three…contact."

The room shuddered again and the spinning drill hesitated momentarily as it crashed into the underwater bedrock, grinding soft stones and pulverising sand.

Claire moved her hand to Cameron's shoulder. "Did we break through?"

"Yeah. It's all good. We're through."

"What now?"

"We wait."

**

Everyone in the canteen leapt to their feet as they felt the Prospero kick into life. "What the fuck is going on?" demanded Captain Anna. "Who the fuck is firing up the drill?"

"Cameron," said Jazmin. "It's got to be. I mean, he's the only one who can operate the control panels, right? It's his baby."

"She's right," said Kurt. "But why isn't he looking for Claire and Roger? Why would he and Bobby decide to just fire up the drill for no reason? You don't suppose he…oh, god…"

"What? What do you mean?" asked Captain Anna.

"It's obvious, isn't it?" asked Betty. "They got to him. One of the last spiders must have gotten to Cameron, and now they're making him fire up the Prospero. You know why, right?"

"Shit. They want reinforcements."

"Bingo. I'll head down to the control room, see if I can't talk some sense into him. Kurt, you come with me. We might need some muscle."

The large geologist looked sceptical. "I'm not exactly Arnold Schwarzenegger."

"No, but you're big, and Cameron's gotta be the least fit guy I ever laid my eyes on. I'll grab weapons."

"Hold fire, hold your fire!" shouted Anna, slapping her fist against the table. "I give the orders here, not you, Harper. You two have already been bitten, and we don't know if it's possible that you might have a relapse of some kind, so we split the groups up. You and I will go and sort out Cameron's little drilling operation. Kurt and Jazmin can go and get on the radio, and get a message through to Icecap. We need their big guns. I don't know what they have at their disposal, but we either need help, or we need to get out of here as soon as possible. Understood?"

"Aye-aye, Captain," said Kurt. "Is the radio tuned in already? Again, it's not really my forte. I was just here to analyse the rocks, you see…"

"No, but there's a print out of the main frequencies pinned to the wall just above it. You should be able to piece it together from there."

Kurt nodded his understanding, and gestured for Jazmin to follow him up to Captain Anna's office.

"Yo, Jazmin!" called Betty. Jazmin turned back and caught the pack of cigarettes the engineer threw her. "Just in case it's a while before you see me again."

"Meet back here?" asked Jazmin.

Anna nodded. "It's where the Twinkies and the *Street Fighter* machine is. Where else would I be?"

Jazmin flashed a smile at them, and then hurried after Kurt.

Once the door had banged shut, Anna flashed a mischievous smile at Betty. "You *are* sweet on her."

"Oh, please. She's about ten years younger than me."

"Still…"

Betty ignored her and rummaged in the kitchen area. She pulled out several meat knives and cleavers and lay them on the counter.

"Betty, this seems a little extreme. I don't want to end up knifing Cameron."

"Don't you? Really?"

"Well, there have been times that I've considered it, but the jail time puts me off."

"The knives aren't for Cam, Claire and whoever else. They're for our arthropod friends."

Anna looked confused. "So, what do we do about the crew that have been compromised?"

Betty placed a crème brûlée blowtorch on the countertop with a thud. She flicked the igniter a few times, and smiled when an inch of blue flame hissed out.

"If a little burn from a radiator worked on me, and cigarette burns woke everyone else, I think it's safe to say Cameron can take a swipe from this."

Anna took the torch which a chuckle. "You're a bad influence on me, Betty Harper."

"I'm a bad influence on everybody."

SIXTEEN

Kurt and Jazmin dashed into Captain Anna's office and Kurt quickly dashed off all the paperwork and discarded coffee cups that had accumulated in front of the radio transmitter. Truth be told, Kurt didn't think that the radio had been used in all the time he'd been there. These days the scheduled arrivals and departures on the Black Hawk were arranged weeks or months in advance, by e-mail. The thick layer of dust on the radio's microphone was a testament to the equipment's obsolescence.

Jazmin looked aghast at the antique equipment before her. "How the hell do we even get this to work?"

Kurt hit the main power switch and the radio crackled into life. He jabbed a finger at a laminated piece of paper pinned to the wall above it. "The Captain said that the frequencies are all up here. We should just be able to dial in, transmit a message and – hopefully - the Icecap base at McMurdo should pick us up."

Jazmin nodded. "Okay…give it a try."

Kurt dialled in the correct frequency, grabbed the handset and pressed the main "talk" button. "Tempest Outpost, Tempest Outpost, Icecap McMurdo, over."

Static greeted them. "Tempest Outpost, Tempest Outpost, Icecap McMurdo. Over."

Jazmin's heart leapt when after what seemed like an hour, a crackly voice at the other end responded. "Icecap McMurdo receiving. Over."

"This is Doctor Kurt Townsend, we require assistance. Over."

"Acknowledged, Tempest Outpost. What can we do for you? Over."

Kurt turned to Jazmin. "What do we tell them?"

Jazmin didn't know what to say. "Uh…can't we just tell them the truth?"

"Tell them that we dug up some fossils that turned out to be scientifically impossible tarantulas and that they have telepathic powers?"

"Okay, when you put it like that, it sounds silly."

The radio crackled again. "Are you receiving, Tempest Outpost? What can we do for you? Over."

Kurt depressed the talk button. "Affirmative, Icecap McMurdo. Stand-by. Over."

Jazmin tapped him on the arm. "Tell them we have a serious problem in the boiler room, and one man is injured. They'll have to send people – engineers and medical. To be honest, I don't care if they're nuns! We just need more people."

Kurt nodded. He turned back to grab the handset and let out a strangled cry as he saw the tarantula that now squatted atop it. Its front legs flew up and its teeth opened wide in a display of aggression. Kurt fell backwards crushing the chair beneath him. Jazmin looked around the table in desperation, looking for a weapon, something heavy she could crush it with. The tarantula, seeming to sense her panic tensed its back legs and leapt forward.

At the last moment, she grabbed hold of a sheaf of papers, and held it up like a shield. The spider landed full force on it, and hurriedly clambered up. She screamed as she saw the long, pale legs creep over the top of the paper, dropping it in revulsion. Before she could stamp on it, the spider scurried out and up the wall. It turned rapidly and leapt back towards her.

From out of nowhere, Kurt stepped between them, a piece of the broken chair held like a baseball bat in his hands. He swung and missed, and the spider instead landed on his chest. He brushed at it, panicked, trying to get it off, but it dodged all his attempts.

"Jazmin! Help!"

Suddenly, the spider pulled its abdomen upwards like a scorpion's tail, and an inch long barb shot out, like a wasp's stinger from hell. The spider hissed and thrust downwards, the barb stabbing deep into Kurt's stomach. He screamed, and Jazmin joined him.

Kurt dropped to his knees, and the spider stabbed him twice more before dropping to the floor and making another aggressive display at Jazmin. Jazmin stepped backwards, her eyes flying to

Kurt. Kurt let out a low groaning noise that faded away to nothing, then fell sideways onto the floor, dead.

The spider hissed at Jazmin once more, and she bolted from the room, locked the door behind her, and ran for the canteen.

***

Anna knew that the door to the control room would be locked, but she felt a need to try it anyway. She cursed under her breath and banged on it hard, shouting to be heard over the industrial noise of the Prospero burrowing beneath them. "Cameron? Open up, it's the Captain."

The door unlocked with a click and slowly opened to reveal the pale and disheveled face of Claire, peering through a small gap. "Yes, Captain?"

"And where the hell have you been? You know we've had search parties out looking for you? What the fuck have you been up to?"

"I don't know."

"Open the damn door, Claire," interrupted Betty, her grip tightening around the cleaver in her hand. "We need to get into the control room."

"Cameron says you can't come in."

"Is he in there with you?"

"Yes."

Betty looked at Anna. "Torch her."

"Sorry, Claire," said Anna, shoving the door hard, and swinging the blowtorch up toward her. Claire yelped and fell backwards, letting out a scream and dodging the flame. Anna swept her gaze around the room, immediately spotting Cameron operating the control panel, completely oblivious both to their entry and Claire's cry. She dashed toward him, and didn't see Roger hiding behind the door.

Betty called out a warning, but too late.

Roger stepped forward and swung the fire extinguisher at Captain Anna's head. To Betty, the world seemed to drag into slow motion, as though someone had put their finger on a record while it was spinning. She saw the solid metal rim of the base of the extinguisher crash down and into the crown of Anna's skull. She saw blood and lumps of bone and flesh spray upwards. The Captain half-turned and Betty managed to catch her gaze for a nanosecond before her eyes rolled upwards and she started to fall. Then, it was as though the finger had been lifted from the vinyl and the Captain collapsed to the floor. Chairs and desks blocked Betty's view, but she could see her foot twitching involuntarily.

"Roger! What the fuck are you doing?" Betty screamed, tears leaping instantly to her eyes.

Roger said nothing, and brought the fire extinguisher down once again, with a sickening crunch. Anna's black leather ankle boot stopped twitching. Roger wiped the blood spray from his face and looked back over to Betty. She took a step back, her grip tightening around the meat cleaver. Roger advanced on her slowly, still holding the gore encrusted fire extinguisher. Betty threw up at the sight of the Captain's blonde hair stuck to its base. Wiping her mouth, she started backing towards the door, hoping for an escape.

Cameron still worked at the control panel, totally undistracted. Roger advanced slowly, obviously wary of the cleaver in her hand. She was reaching behind her for the door when, suddenly, Claire grabbed her from behind, and tried to throw her to the ground. Betty yelled and ran backwards as fast as she could, barreling into the wall, crushing Claire against it. Claire let out a grunt and sunk her teeth into Betty's neck. Betty yelled through clenched teeth against the pain and slammed her into the wall again and again. Eventually Claire's grip loosened and she dropped to the floor. Betty kicked her in the head for good measure, and Claire fell still.

She turned and saw that Roger was almost on her, the fire extinguisher held high. Screaming in a panic she swung the cleaver hard into his side. He let out a grunt and dropped his weapon, falling to one knee. Betty wondered if this would be enough to wake him from his hellish hypnotism, but he didn't even clasp a hand to the wound, and instead just rose up to his feet like a zombie from a Fulci movie. Betty turned and ran from the room, hoping that Kurt and Jazmin would have gotten through to the Black Hawk, and would be waiting in the canteen.

In the now still and quiet room, Cameron's eyes remained glued to the screen of the control panel. The Prospero drill bit had penetrated deeper than before, and now it was time to use the "icebreaker". He hit the ignition, and operated a feature that he had never thought he would have cause to use, as the main action of the drill had proven much stronger than he had anticipated.

The chambers inside the drill fired up and a jet of superheated air, originally designed to melt large blocks of ice, blasted from the tip, heating the Antarctic water below, causing the sea to bubble and even the occasional wisp of steam to ghost across the surface.

The egg chamber below began to heat up, and the contents of those eggs began to stir.

Cameron stretched out his legs, put his hands behind his head and smiled. He'd done a good job. He'd designed a wonderful tool.

The room was silent until Roger finally lost enough blood and collapsed to the floor. Later, Claire stirred a little, but for the most part, it was just Cameron and the Prospero, enjoying each other's company.

SEVENTEEN

Betty and Jazmin burst through into the canteen almost simultaneously, from opposite doors, and with one glance at each other they both knew that things had gone very wrong. They walked slowly to the central table, shell shocked. Jazmin's eyes flickered to the blood stained meat cleaver in Betty's hand, and she asked, "Cameron?"

Betty shook her head. "No. He's alive, and still working the drill. Roger killed the Captain, and I killed Roger. At least, I think I did."

They both slumped into the hard, uncomfortable plastic chairs, and Jazmin put a hand on her arm. "It's okay. You did what you had to do."

"Did you get through to Icecap McMurdo? Is the Black Hawk coming?"

Jazmin looked apologetic. "Kind of. We got through, and they knew we needed assistance, but before we could tell them exactly what we needed, one of the spiders killed Kurt. I ran."

"The spiders can kill now? I thought they just had that telepathic venom?"

Jazmin started crying. "They have something like a wasp's stinger. It's hidden most of the time, but Kurt got stabbed with it two or three times. Then he died. And I ran."

Betty rubbed her eyes with the balls of her hands and groaned.

"Is it just you and me left now?" asked Jazmin.

"Cameron and maybe Claire are still alive, but they're...spider brained. I don't know about Bobby. I didn't see him. He could be dead, or hive-minded, or he could be holding up somewhere, like you and I."

Jazmin wiped the tears from her eyes. "Okay. Okay. So what are we going to do now?"

"We're going back to the radio room together, killing that spider, and calling Icecap McMurdo for help."

"I...I can't go back in there."

"You'd rather sit here alone?"

Betty stood up, stuck the cleaver in the side pocket of her combats and walked over to the other side of the canteen. "Let's explore the kitchen some more. We need weapons, and this is the best place we're going to find them."

***

After what seemed like forever, Cameron finally stopped the hypnotically spinning drill and sat back. The largest of the spiders sat at the console next to him, the light from the setting sun reflecting red in its many eyes. It twitched and flexed its fangs and legs and let out a little hissing sound.

They came slowly at first, one or two…then a clutch of five, their white chitinous bodies standing out bright against the dirty gunmetal of the Prospero. Awoken from their eon long slumber, the ice spiders began to climb up to claim the drilling rig. It was only a matter of seconds before it seemed as though hundreds of them were running up the drill, covering it in a rolling, scampering white mass. Yet, more still poured forth from the sea.

Cameron smiled. His drill had done well. He would change the world with his invention.

***

Approaching the door to Captain Anna's office, large meat tenderiser in hand, Betty stopped Jazmin with a gesture. "You hear that?"

"What?"

"The drill's stopped."

"Why would it stop?"

"I don't know. Cameron must have switched it off."

Jazmin held her rolling pin tightly in both hands, the handle of some kitchen scissors just poking out of her jacket pocket. "Do you think he's…?"

"No. Something else is going on. Come on. We need to get to that radio."

Reaching the door, Betty looked through the glass window to the inside. Straight away she saw Kurt, slumped on the floor, his face toward her, contorted into a terrified and pained rictus. She swept her gaze across the rest of the room, feeling her heart leap into her throat when she saw the spider sitting on the radio, the handset now obscured under a thick web. She rested her hand on the doorknob, intending to rush the spider and crush it with the steak hammer, when Jazmin screamed and she practically jumped out of her skin.

She saw Jazmin, pale as snow, pointing toward the main window with her finger, and when Betty saw what the girl was pointing at, she thought that her own heart might explode.

The Prospero was covered – from the high chuck at the base of the helipad, all the way down to the water – in a seething, rolling white mass of the ice spiders. When she was a child, Betty had seen a dead dog on the beach, and it had been covered in little crabs, all feeding on the dead flesh, acting as one large mass of pincers and eyes and skittering legs. This was like that, only a hundred times more macabre and a hundred times more unearthly.

"Jesus...how many are there?" she breathed.

"Thousands," whimpered Jazmin. "My god...we have to get out of here."

"Yeah. Yeah, we do."

"We need the Black Hawk."

"There's a spider sat on the radio, but there's only one of them. You throw the door open and I'll rush it with the hammer. Then, you and I are going to radio for help."

"Okay. I'm scared, Betty. There are thousands of them out there. What can the chopper do?"

"It can get us out of here, it can get someone else to see what's happening here. Then they can come back, prepared, and they can deal with the spiders. Are you going to help me?"

"Yes."

"Good. Now, take the door handle and – on three – throw it open, and I'll take care of the rest. Can you do that?"

Jazmin nodded her agreement and took a shaky hold of the door handle. She turned her tear stained eyes to Betty, and waited for the signal.

"Ready? One...two...*three!*"

Jazmin threw the door open and Betty charged in with the steak hammer. The spider saw her and threw its legs up and its fangs wide. It turned a little to face her, but before it could leap, Betty smashed it sideways on with the spiky wooden mallet, and the foul creature went flying sideways into a filing cabinet, exploding into shards of chitin and a strange black grit, like a crushed pencil. "Spider's down!" Betty called back to Jazmin, who followed her in.

Betty swept the spider's web from the radio handset and jabbered out a communication. Their spirits lifted when Icecap McMurdo answered. "Receiving you, Tempest Outpost. How can we help? Over."

"We need immediate evacuation. Samples we brought up were...contaminated. We have crew dead and crew poisoned. We need medical assistance and a clean-up team. Over."

"Acknowledged, Tempest Outpost. I'll see what's available, and get back to you. Stand by. Over."

"Acknowledged. Standing by. Over."

Jazmin played nervously with her fingers and watched the spiders through the window. Some of them were spreading out from the drill now and crawling across the underside of the helipad, down gantries and across windows. "Betty, there are more of them. And they're climbing onto the rig."

Betty joined her side, and watched with her. "You're right. There must be nearly a thousand by now."

"Some are larger, too. That one must be twelve inches across."

"You're not wrong. Ugly little fuckers, aren't they?"

The radio crackled and burst into life. "Tempest Outpost, are you receiving? Over."

Betty ran to the handset and grabbed it. "Tempest Outpost, receiving. Go ahead, Icecap McMurdo, over."

"UH-60 Black Hawk and medical crew is readying now. They should be with you in approximately one hour."

Betty's heart sank. She knew they were miles from anywhere, but had been hoping for a miracle. "Acknowledged, Icecap McMurdo. Thank you. Over."

"Sit tight, Tempest Outpost, and watch for them from the helipad. Over and out."

Jazmin couldn't take her eyes from the window. "We're going to have to hold up here for an hour, then make a dash for the helipad."

Jazmin couldn't take her eyes from the undulating mass of spiders that were now leaping onto gantry ways and climbing up ladders, some spinning webs as they jumped, which others of them then used to climb across.

"I don't know there'll still be a rig here in half an hour! We could all be webbed up. Betty, I don't think we're going to make it. I don't want to die here, Betty! I was just supposed to do filing and clean beakers in the lab! I can't do this."

Betty pressed the rolling pin back into Jazmin's sweaty palms. "You will. We both will. We just have to hold out and we'll be just fine."

Her heart leapt into her mouth as there came a tapping on the door's window. "Jazmin? Are you in there? It's Claire. I'm...I'm all right now. When Betty clocked me, I woke up. Cameron's fixated on the drill. He didn't notice me sneak out. I saw Anna. That was... Are you in there? I thought I could hear you."

"Fuck..." whispered Betty.

"What?" hissed back Jazmin. "She says she's okay!"

"We can't believe her!"

"If she's telling the truth, we can't leave her to die!"

Betty was about to respond when a percussive vibration ran through the whole of the rig, and her first thought was that something had exploded.

EIGHTEEN

The two of them ran to the window, looking out to the Prospero and the vast army of terrible spiders that were crawling even faster now, as though some sense of agitation or excitement was sweeping over them.

"What are they doing?" whispered Jazmin.

Betty felt her arm hairs rise up. "They're…they're hatching. I remember seeing it once. When I was a kid we found a spider with an egg sac in our garage, and I saw it hatch. The spiders just pour out in a near constant stream. They just…flow. It was amazing, they just…"

They were both thrown sideways by the force of what felt like another explosion. Betty fell hard, bruising her lower back, and Jazmin hit a desk, sending papers flying. "What the hell was that?"

"I don't know. Could it be the boiler room? That was where we thought the nest was," grunted Betty.

"No, it's coming from the other direction. It's…oh god…"

Jazmin turned pale, and Betty had to grab a hold of her arm and shake her to get her attention. "What? What is it?"

"What did you say about what you found in the garage?"

"An egg sac?"

"Yeah. Describe it."

"It was, like, small, and white and encased webbing, and full of little tiny eggs that hatched really, really super-duper tiny spiders. What are you getting at?"

"*Where* was it?"

Betty didn't follow, but Jazmin was obviously upset. "I told you. In my family's garage."

Jazmin grabbed a hold of Betty's jacket and whispered hoarsely into her face. "Was it hanging from the ceiling? Embedded in a web?"

"No, the mother was carrying it on a...No. It can't be..."

The two of them jumped up to the window, and peered through the spray and encroaching darkness. There, on the outside of one of the corner pylons supporting the main structure of Tempest Outpost, a colossal spider's leg, easily the length of a train, was straining into it. As it did so, the rig shuddered under its weight, and another limb rose up from the deep black ocean, this one reaching and stretching blindly out for purchase.

Jazmin's eyes filled with tears and she whispered: "We're not going to last an hour."

Betty forced herself away from the window. "Don't look. Just, let's focus on getting up to the helipad. We can wait for the Black Hawk there, and we'll be better positioned to keep an eye out for any of the spiders. There's nowhere for them to hide up there. We can improvise some flame throwers maybe?"

"How do we do that?"

"Grab a gas canister from stores, maybe? I don't know!"

The banging came at the door again, and Claire said: "I can hear you in there! Open the door and let me in!"

"We're going to have to deal with her," whispered Betty. "There's no other way out of here."

"What do we do?" asked Jazmin. "Do we kill her?"

The knocking came again, louder and more insistent. "Please! Let me in! There are hundreds of them out here! I need you!"

Betty cursed. "Fuck it. No. We take her with us."

"Are you *serious*?"

"Yeah, I'm fucking serious. If she's lucid, and has broken their control, then we can't just stab her, and leaving her here with these spiders is as good as killing her. We...we have to take her with us."

Jazmin tried to grab Betty's sleeve as the woman went to answer the door, but missed and simply watched her, terrified. Betty glanced back at her one last time before unbolting the door and opening it slowly. Claire pushed the door open wide and crashed straight into her, knocking Betty to the floor and landing on top of her. Betty screamed to Jazmin to close the door, and she rushed for it, slamming it shut, catching and exploding two spiders in the doorframe. She slammed the bolt home hard.

Claire had staggered to her feet and was looking around, dazed and confused. Betty got up and shoved her down into a chair. "Okay, talk...how did you get up here?"

"I...I don't remember. I woke up in the control room, and those things were just *everywhere*. They'd covered everything. The only light came from where the ceiling lights glowed through their webbing, and from the screen of the control desk. I could hear Cameron moving around, but I couldn't see him. I just crawled out of there, and I made my way up here. I tried the canteen first, but you weren't there, and then I just wandered. I thought I could hear you in here, so I tried the door. Thank you. Thank you for letting me in. Thank you so much. I thought I was going to die."

"Okay. You were hypnotised by the spiders somehow. We can't figure out quite how it works, but basically, they influence your thoughts and you then have no memory of it. They got me, at one time, but there's a way to break you out of it."

"What? No. I'm fine. I'm fine now! I promise!"

Betty nodded to Jazmin, and then pushed Claire from her chair onto the floor. Jazmin jumped on top of her and pulled her arm out straight. Claire struggled, drumming her feet on the floor and pleaded for them to stop. "Wait! What are you doing?"

"Sorry about this, Claire. We have to be sure."

"What? What's happening?"

She felt Betty grab her hand and Jazmin's palm slap over her mouth, and then she heard the metallic ping of Betty's Zippo opening.

***

The three of them pushed open the door into the store room, Claire still whimpering about her burned hand. "Grab anything you can find as a weapon," Betty whispered to Claire, before turning back to Jazmin. "Help me find something that we can make a flame thrower from."

Claire went shuffling off into the darkness, and Jazmin tugged on Betty's sleeve. "I've been thinking, and…might that be a really bad idea? I mean, didn't heat accelerate these things? All the time they were asleep down there, they were deep in the freezing cold ocean. I'm…really not sure I want to warm them up more. It's like the stinger thing they killed Kurt with. Maybe that only became an option once they warmed up. You douse them with fire and they could sprout wings for all we know!"

"Fuck. Yeah, you're right. Okay, we ditch the flame thrower. Just grab some supplies, and any weapons you can find. Two minutes, and we're heading up to the helipad."

They had hidden in the Captain's office for half an hour, and only decided to make a run for it when more and more spiders started crawling across the window, and they were worried they'd be spotted. The occasional rhythmic thuds told them that mother spider was still climbing the rig and their only hope was that they'd be on the Black Hawk out of there before she reached the helipad.

Claire rejoined them, holding a fire axe. "Okay. Let's go."

"Hold on. Jazmin's grabbing some things."

Jazmin had disappeared down one of the aisles, and they could hear her pulling out boxes and packets. Betty wondered what she could be looking for.

Finally, they heard a cry of satisfaction, and Jazmin jogged back to them, carrying a fire extinguisher. She handed it to Betty. "Here. Carbon dioxide. Reverse flame thrower."

Betty had a brief flashback to Roger, holding the extinguisher above the fallen Anna Morris, but pushed it from her mind. "Jazmin, you're a genius! There's got to be two or three of these on the way to the helipad, right? We could easily take one each, and use those to hold them off on the helipad until the Black Hawk arrives."

Jazmin's eyes opened wide and looked past Betty. Claire screamed.

Betty spun around and saw a tarantula the size of a dinner plate hanging by a thread in the middle of the door back out of the store room. Betty yanked the pin out of the extinguisher and pulled the nozzle straight. The spider let out a weird chittering sound, and Betty squeezed the handle. With a hollow, gasping bark, the carbon dioxide belched forth, obscuring the spider. When the fog dissipated, the spider had withdrawn back up to the top of the doorframe, pulling all of its legs up close to its body. Claire dashed forward and smashed the spider with the back of the axe head. It exploded into shards and dust, which dissipated into the corridor.

"I hate these things," she muttered. "Let's get the fuck out of here."

Betty smiled and was about to agree, when the floor tilted beneath them.

NINETEEN

Ducking out of Captain Anna's office, they turned a sharp left and began jogging along the corridor. Betty threw open a pair of fire doors leading through to a flight of stairs, and they all took them two at a time. Shoving aside another pair of doors they re-entered the corridor system, and came to a dead stop as they turned toward the quickest route to the helipad.

The entire corridor was covered with webbing.

"How the hell did they get up here so fast?" asked Jazmin.

"They've had the run of the air ducts this whole time," said Betty. "They could have started work on this hours ago. I guess they knew this was an entry way, and instinctively they wanted to cover it up; like ants hiding the entrance to their nest with a stone."

"Or a funnel web," said Claire. "This might not be a defensive fortification. It could be a snare. Like a trap door spider."

Jazmin tugged at Betty's sleeve. "We need to get out of here. We don't know how many of them are watching us right now."

Betty nodded and whispered. "Yeah, you're right. Okay, we need to go. Claire? You coming with us?"

"Yes, of course. Sorry."

"This way."

Betty ducked them into a wood panelled cloakroom, and pulled on a thick parka. "Come on. We'll cut across to the other side via the gantry ways."

"Are you kidding?" said Jazmin. "There has to be a thousand spiders out there!"

"Yeah. Plus Kumonga. But I'd rather take a run across out there."

"Why?" asked Claire. "What kind of thinking is that?"

"Because it's cold out. It's the Antarctic. Most of the time, out there, it's barely above sub-zero. They'll be slow. They'll be stupid. In here, they're warmed up and full of beans."

Jazmin pulled on a coat and threw another to Claire. "She's right. They'll be dopey. Slow. Let's go for it."

Claire tugged up the zipper, and threw the hood over her head. "This stinks. Whose was this?"

"It's a communal. Not everyone had their own. Just the regulars," said Betty, feeling a lump in her throat when she found a Twinkie in the pocket of hers.

Stepping outside, the cold hit them like a brick wall, blasting the breath from their lungs. This was a good thing, as all three of them would have screamed when they saw the monster spider climbing up the legs and struts of the oil rig. It was easily the size of the rig itself, its massive body impossibly huge. It was the mother of all spiders. Betty could see its fangs moving above them; its vile, bloated abdomen nearer, just about clearing the water now, pulsing and swaying. A vile groaning sound screeched across to them and they saw a gantry under one of its legs bend chaotically.

"It's too heavy for the rig!" shouted Jazmin, over the wind. "It'll pull the whole thing down!"

"There's no time for this!" shouted Betty, pulling them into motion. "We've got to run!"

The three of them jogged across the gantry ways, running along the opposite side from the colossal spider creature, although all threw worried, nervous glances in its direction. One of its legs shifted again and the entire gantry rocked ten degrees to the right, eliciting screams from all of them as they grabbed hold of the safety railing. Several of the spiders on the floor – which they had been carefully running around, and occasionally kicking away – were not so lucky, and went tumbling into the cold, black water below.

The distance was further than any of them had anticipated, and Betty stopped for a breather when they reached the halfway point. The spiders around them didn't seem to notice their presence. "I must have been right about the cold," she gasped around lungfuls of air. "They're really slow – they don't even seem to have noticed us."

"Maybe. Maybe they're just waiting for *her*," replied Jazmin. "It worries me that she's climbing up top. What if the Black Hawk can't land because she's sat up there?"

"I'm more worried that there won't be a helipad in a few minutes," said Claire. "That thing is just…too heavy for Tempest Outpost."

"If the rig is going to collapse, there's nothing we can do about it," said Betty. "Come on."

They jogged the remainder of the way, and once they had reached the far end, they almost flew up several flights of stairs, never letting go of the handrails, as the entire structure was now shuddering and lurching with each footfall of the goliath arachnid. At last they reached the top, threw open the fire door and…looked into blackness.

"The lights are all out," whispered Claire. "Why are all the lights out?"

"My guess?" asked Betty. "The Ungoliant out there pulled a wire or crushed a fuse box or something."

Betty flicked on a torch and swept its beam down the dark hallway. There were no signs of any webs or spiders anywhere. "Come on. Looks like the coast is clear."

Jazmin felt a strange sensation as they reached the next cloakroom leading to the helipad. It had only been a few days since she had landed here and come through that door with the Captain and Kurt, and now they were both dead, and she was running from a Godzilla sized spider that was threatening to collapse Tempest Outpost underneath their feet.

She caught Claire's eye, and it was obvious that she was feeling something similar. "Never a dull moment, huh?" she asked.

Betty opened the door, and it was like opening an oven door. They all recoiled from the heat that gusted around them. Betty scanned her torch around the floor of the darkened room, and saw that all five of the fan heaters had been turned on full blast. She swept her torch up and gasped out loud. There stood Cameron Barnett, with one of the spiders riding his shoulder. She swept the beam around and counted ten more of the things crawling up the walls.

Cameron gave them an eerie smile. "Three lovely ladies...coming in to meet mother?"

Betty stepped forward, torch held up high in an attempt to lighten the room. She could make out the door on the other side, which led out onto the helipad. It hadn't been webbed up, and she couldn't make out any spiders keeping an obvious watch on it. "Hello, Cameron. What's going on?"

Claire and Jazmin followed her in cautiously, keeping close together. Cameron rubbed his lips with the back of his hand and shook his head a little. "Nothing. Nothing much. I just...ran the drill."

"You did. Looks like you've made quite the discovery."

Another screech of metal and a distant explosion meant that the monster spider had clambered up another floor of the rig. "She's impressive, isn't she? And you know what the best part is?"

"What's the best part?"

"The babies."

"What about the babies?" asked Betty. She was still holding the fire extinguisher and really wished that she'd ditched it for a more conventional weapon.

"Well, isn't it obvious?" he smiled. "Every one of these babies has the potential to grow just as big as their mother here. It's not just a geological discovery, Betty. It's a zoological one! A whole new species, previously unknown to mankind has awoken from hibernation!"

A spider had crept a little too close for comfort, and she nudged it away sharply with her boot. She was now only about a foot away from Cameron. "So, what's the plan now?"

Cameron shrugged. "Keep them warm. Keep them fed. See what happens to the world now a creature from the Hadean period is back."

"Okay…that is an interesting proposition. We're waiting on the Black Hawk, Cameron. Why don't you come with us, and tell all the Icecap dudes at McMurdo about it? We can do a full report, and then they'll all come back with a full science team."

"No."

"Why not?"

"Because that's not what she wants."

"We're leaving, and you should come too."

The spider on his shoulder flexed its front legs and teeth and she knew that it was about to leap onto her. She brought the fire extinguisher nozzle up and gave it a blast of carbon dioxide. The thing screeched and fell from Cameron's shoulder onto the floor. Claire brought her boot down on it hard and the thing exploded.

Cameron's face twisted into cartoon rage and he let out an actual snarl. Betty was ready to defend herself, when out of nowhere Jazmin rugby tackled him hard. For a small girl, she was surprisingly strong, and Cameron was decidedly less than sporty. He took the hit badly, and Jazmin managed to push him all the way across the room, through the door and out onto the helipad.

Freezing cold air filled the small room and the remaining spiders huddled away from it in corners, ceilings and crevices. Betty and Claire raced after Jazmin and Cameron, just in time to see a long, arachnoid leg reach up and over the far side of the helipad, and begin to pull the monster up.

TWENTY

Jazmin hurriedly disentangled herself from the fallen Cameron and looked around the helipad. After being inside, the sound of the waves and the wind was almost deafening, and she felt the change like a physical shock. Betty and Claire scooped her up by her armpits and set her on her feet. "You okay?" asked Betty, frantically.

"Yeah, I'm fine, I…" her gaze was drawn suddenly to the second of the mother spider's legs clawing up onto the helipad, and gouging into the concrete. Slowly, the monster's head rose up into view, its vile, pale pink eyes set in that horrendous black head, scanning for movement – for prey. "Holy shit, we're fucked."

Claire clutched her fire axe tightly and looked all around her as dozens of the ice spiders started to crawl across the helipad towards them. The chill was obviously still affecting them, but under the influence of their vile mother, they seemed to be emboldened. "It sure looks that way."

Cameron groaned below them and Betty put her foot down on his neck. "Stay down, Spider-Man."

"Wait!" called Claire. "Up there! You see it?"

Jazmin turned her gaze upwards and saw a flashing red light in the distance. "The chopper!" she screamed. "It's the Black Hawk!"

Jazmin stamped on two spiders that had gotten too close, their bodies exploding into what resembled bone chips and graphite. "Looks like we might get out of this after all. You know what I'm going to do when I get back to civilisation?"

Betty blasted the spiders on her side with a hollow bark of the extinguisher. "What's that?"

"I'm going to have a six pack, I'm going to smoke a jay, and I'm going to watch *all* the goddamn *Poltergeist* movies."

Betty laughed, and didn't tell her that she should probably stop at the first one. "That sounds like a plan. Mind if I join you?"

"I was pretty much banking on it."

Jazmin's laugh turned into a scream as the floor shifted below them, to a ten-degree slant towards the vile spider monster, which flexed its bus sized pedipalps and its building sized fangs into anticipation of its first meal in a very long time. Betty fell hard on her backside, and Cameron rolled out from underneath her, slipping and sliding down towards the monster. For a moment, Betty thought he was going to slide right into its jaws, but instead he slipped between the beast and the struts of the rig, and simply disappeared from view with a scream.

Jazmin grabbed hold of a nearby strut and tried to get her bearings as the rig shuddered and shook under the terrible weight of the prehistoric monster. She saw Betty grab hold of a railing, but Claire was not so lucky. She slipped and fell, and it was only the quick action of Betty stamping on the hood of her borrowed parka that stopped her from following Cameron down into the water below.

Getting her balance back, Claire slowly kicked and scrabbled her way upright, and held tight onto the railing next to Betty. Jazmin looked up again and while the Black Hawk was much nearer, she was no longer sure that it would be able to land on the helipad at all, given its highly precarious angle. The hollow bark of the fire extinguisher brought her attention back to ground level and the sight of Betty desperately spraying away twenty, perhaps thirty, of the ice spiders.

Claire reached out to an orange box secured to the wall, of the type that might hold a fire axe, or other potentially useful weapon. "Jazmin!" she called out. "Get over here as soon and as safely as you can."

The monster spider threw up another of its legs over the side, and Jazmin tried her best to suppress a scream of terror, although even if she had let rip it would have been lost in the Antarctic wind. Hand over hand she made her way around the railing and hanging bits of debris to Betty and Claire.

Claire pulled the bright orange flare gun from the box, cocked it and fired it onto the ground about six feet away from them. The yellow white light lit them up in the darkness, and

Jazmin convinced herself that she could actually hear the chopping of the Black Hawks rotors as it made its way toward them.

Several of the spiders were also drawn by the fire and some of them even tried leaping towards them in an effort to sink their teeth in, but they were pushed back by Betty's fire extinguisher, although she was worried that too much blasting would put out the very signal flare that they needed so badly.

Another sickening crunch came as the mother spider brought up another leg over the lip and Jazmin did let out a scream this time. Just as she thought that she was going to go tumbling head over heels into the foul thing's maw, or into the dark water below, the entire helipad was lit up by the searchlight of the Black Hawk. A voice called down to them through a loudhailer, but it was too indistinct or the wind was too strong for them to hear anything at all.

There was a rattle and a clatter, and a wound steel ladder was thrown down from the Black Hawk. Betty shoved Claire and Jazmin towards it first of all. "You two go, I'll hold off these guys with the extinguisher."

"Don't be a hero! Get going with us!" shouted Jazmin.

"Will you fucking go, already?" demanded Betty.

Claire was already several rungs up the ladder, and Jazmin followed hot on her heels. The Black Hawk was forced to bank sharply as the rig shuddered under the weight of the spider once more. Betty's heart sank as she saw it pull thirty feet or more away from her. She blasted the surrounding area, and couldn't help but notice how light the fire extinguisher was getting.

Up on the Black Hawk, Jazmin shouted at the man who helped her aboard. "There's still one of us down there. You need to go back for her!"

The man nodded. "We're going to swoop back as soon as we can, but that…you saw that thing, right?"

"Yeah. I saw it. Doesn't this thing carry any missiles or bombs or shit like that?"

"Military ones, for sure. This is a privately owned chopper. All we've got is a winch, horsepower and a bad-ass look."

"Fuck it. Go for her now!"

Betty looked up as the Black Hawk and its ladder swung back towards her. She reached up and grabbed it just as it passed by, gripping with all her might. At the exact same moment, the mother spider brought the bulk of its weight up onto the helipad, and the entire Tempest Outpost let out a screech, a crash and a groan, and began to fall sideways into the ocean. Betty let out a scream as she felt her shoulder dislocate from the pressure of carrying her entire body weight. She dropped the extinguisher and desperately gripped onto another rung. Up above her, the ladder began to be winched in, until the Icecap co-pilot, Jazmin and Claire could pull her into the cargo bay.

Betty fell over onto her side, only partly conscious. Through the moonlight she saw the mother spider and all of Tempest Outpost collapse, crashing with an almighty noise back into the ocean. She thought for a moment of all the friends she had lost over the last two days, and mourned them. She also thought that she had come very close to being permanently under the sway of the spiders herself, and it was only a happy accident that had broken her from the spell. She looked over at Claire and saw that the same thought had occurred to her, too.

They watched the rig collapse and crash downwards for as long as it remained in sight, but there was no sign of the mother spider. A few small fires had broken out where electrics or fuel supplies had malfunctioned or been broken open, but there was no big explosion that served as a full stop to their ordeal. Just a limp semi-colon; or perhaps a question mark? Who knew what else was down there? How many of the spiders survived? How many eggs were still down there, waiting to hatch?

Claire rested her hand on her shoulder. "Are you okay? Are you hurt?"

Betty winced. "I think I dislocated my shoulder, but nothing too bad, no. You?"

"I'm fine."

Betty sat up and leaned back against the interior wall, and felt Jazmin pull her into a hug. She rested her head on the young girl's shoulder and closed her eyes as the Black Hawk banked and sped them away to Icecap McMurdo.

THE END

CHECK OUT OTHER GREAT HORROR NOVELS

BLACK FRIDAY
by Michael Hodges

Jared the kleptomaniac, Chike the unemployed IT guy, Patricia the shopaholic, and Jeff the meth dealer are trapped inside a Chicago supermall on Black Friday. Bridgefield Mall empties during a fire alarm, and most of the shoppers drive off into a strange mist surrounding the mall parking lot. They never return. Chike and his group try calling friends and family, but their smart phones won't work, not even Twitter. As the mist creeps closer, the mall lights flicker and surge. Bulbs shatter and spray glass into the air. Unsettling noises are heard from within the mist, as the meth dealer becomes unhinged and hunts the group within the mall. Cornered by the mist, and hunted from within, Chike and the survivors must fight for their lives while solving the mystery of what happened to Bridgefield Mall. Sometimes, a good sale just isn't worth it.

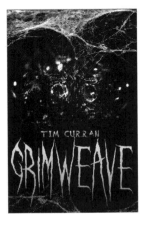

GRIMWEAVE
by Tim Curran

In the deepest, darkest jungles of Indochina, an ancient evil is waiting in a forgotten, primeval valley. It is patient, monstrous, and bloodthirsty. Perfectly adapted to its hot, steaming environment, it strikes silent and stealthy, it chosen prey: human. Now Michael Spiers, a Marine sniper, the only survivor of a previous encounter with the beast, is going after it again. Against his better judgement, he is made part of a Marine Force Recon team that will hunt it down and destroy it.

The hunters are about to become the hunted.

 facebook.com/severedpress
 twitter.com/severedpress

CHECK OUT OTHER GREAT HORROR NOVELS

DEATH CRAWLERS
by Gerry Griffiths

Worldwide, there are thought to be 8,000 species of centipede, of which, only 3,000 have been scientifically recorded. The venom of Scolopendra gigantea—the largest of the arthropod genus found in the Amazon rainforest—is so potent that it is fatal to small animals and toxic to humans. But when a cargo plane departs the Amazon region and crashes inside a national park in the United States, much larger and deadlier creatures escape the wreckage to roam wild, reproducing at an astounding rate. Entomologist, Frank Travis solicits small town sheriff Wanda Rafferty's help and together they investigate the crash site. But as a rash of gruesome deaths befalls the townsfolk of Prospect, Frank and Wanda will soon discover how vicious and cunning these new breed of predators can be. Meanwhile, Jake and Nora Carver, and another backpacking couple, are venturing up into the mountainous terrain of the park. If only they knew their fun-filled weekend is about to become a living nightmare.

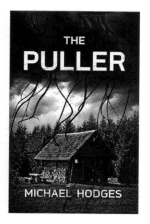

THE PULLER
by Michael Hodges

Matt Kearns has two choices: fight or hide. The creature in the orchard took the rest. Three days ago, he arrived at his favorite place in the world, a remote shack in Michigan's Upper Peninsula. The plan was to mourn his father's death and figure out his life. Now he's fighting for it. An invisible creature has him trapped. Every time Matt tries to flee, he's dragged backwards by an unseen force. Alone and with no hope of rescue, Matt must escape the Puller's reach. But how do you free yourself from something you cannot see?

CHECK OUT OTHER GREAT HORROR NOVELS

MONSTROSITY
by Tim Curran

The Food. It seeped from the ground, a living, gushing, teratogenic nightmare. It contaminated anything that ate it, causing nature to run wild with horrible mutations, creating massive monstrosities that roam the land destroying towns and cities, feeding on livestock and human beings and one another. Now Frank Bowman, an ordinary farmer with no military skills, must get his children to safety. And that will mean a trip through the contaminated zone of monsters, madmen, and The Food itself. Only a fool would attempt it. Or a man with a mission.

THE SQUIRMING
by Jack Hamlyn

You are their hosts.

You are their food.

The parasites came out of nowhere, squirming horrors that enslaved the human race. They turned the population into mindless pack animals, psychotic cannibalistic hordes whose only purpose was to feed them.

Now with the human race teetering at the edge of extinction, extermination teams are fighting back, killing off the parasites and their voracious hosts. Taking them out one by one in violent, bloody encounters.

The future of mankind is at stake.

And time is running out.